And I wish I'd asked why

David Hall

Ian,
Excellent to meet a fellow writer. Best of luck!
A Wootten AKA David Hall.

Electric Monk, an imprint of
Eskdale Publishing
www.antonywootten.co.uk/davidhall.html

Eskdale Publishing, UK

First published in Great Britain in 2014 by Electric Monk, an imprint of Eskdale Publishing, North Yorkshire

www.antonywootten.co.uk

A Catalogue record for this book is available from the British Library.

ISBN: 978-0-9537123-7-3

**Printed and bound in the UK by
York Publishing Services
www.yps-publishing.co.uk**

To my wife, who has a wonderfully wise outlook on life, as illustrated by the following advice she gave me one day when I was feeling stressed about something trivial:
"Don't worry, geese still exist."

Contents

The End

Matthew had been playing with his toys in the nursery: the creaky old rocking horse, the wooden plane, and the dog. He'd been lazing amongst the musty cushions, the sunlight warming his back as it smiled down through the tall windows. He'd been wondering when it would be time for dinner; toying with the idea of riding his new bike around the lawn; dreaming of the faraway places in the big atlas which he loved.

But the room had become cold. His head felt swimmy; he was suddenly aware of being alone, as if everyone in the world had, in that instant, vanished. He moved towards the door, his feet scuffing clumsily on the wooden floor. He felt a dark and nasty dread rising inside him. Why did the house feel so ... *weird?* He heard something: a whisper, a voice that was both familiar and forgotten, and he could not tell what it said, but it was menacing, and he felt as if his skin was turning to ice.

Slowly, he eased the door open. The landing was bright, too bright. The lights burned into his eyes, dizzying him. He put his hand against the wall to steady himself, and again the voice hissed at him, spurring him forwards in fear.

This was not his house.

This landing was long and wide and bright, and the walls were pale, and the carpet soft. He did not know this place. Matthew did not belong here. He had to get out. It

1

was like being a disease inside a giant living thing: the house wanted to get him out, to eject him like vomit. He couldn't get to the staircase quickly enough. His breathing was heavy and frantic, and there was pain clawing at his legs. He wished his father would dash in and save him from this living nightmare; he wished his mother would appear and hold him until the fear was gone.

He began to inch his way down the stairs, desperate to escape, yet afraid to run. Multiple voices now hissed and breathed in his head, wordless, and hateful. He clapped his hands over his ears but that just seemed to trap the voices inside, making them swell and billow in his brain. He cried, and lurched down the steps, violent pain sparking through his knees and up one side of his body. Was he dying? "Mum!" he cried.

He reached the bottom of the stairs and stood in the hallway, unsure of which way to go. Ahead of him was a wide front door, the stained glass window glowing blood red before him. The door was partly open, moving slightly in a sighing breeze. Little ginger leaves tiptoed in and played on the red and black tiles.

And then the door's glass darkened in the shape of an approaching figure. His heart lurched and jerked. He gripped the banister and watched, and the voices roared in his head to a silent crescendo. The approaching figure pushed the door wide and stood, a black shadow in the blinding light behind.

Matthew staggered, almost falling backwards onto the steps. The figure was a windswept woman in a long duffle coat, her hair sticking to her lipstick and clinging to her eye lashes. She eased it away from her face and smiled at him. "Are you ready?" she said. "The car's all packed."

He stared in confusion; he could see she was not to be feared, but who was she? She approached him, head cocked to one side in apparent sympathy. The voices had fallen silent now, as if waiting for him to react; as if a penny was about to drop.

"Come on," she said, taking Matthew's hand gently in hers. A tear had broken and tumbled down her cheek. "It's me, Susie. Your daughter." She looked down at the floor, letting her hair fall into a curtain around her face. When she looked at him again, there were more tears, but the smile was still there; a sympathetic and wise one. "You'll like it in the home, Dad; they'll know exactly how to look after you."

Blood on My Hands

I pressed the accelerator and felt the Volvo surge forwards, the windscreen wipers slashing their way through sheets of rain like a machete through dense undergrowth. I realised I was sweating. This was insane! I never lost my head like this, not when I was in the forces and not in my ... more recent work. I had to get a fucking grip. The narrow road curved beneath a crag and I felt the car twitch as the tyres skittered slightly on the wet tarmac. I glanced at the clock as the car straightened, and I opened up the power again, pressing forwards towards the town. I had less than eight minutes.

On the passenger seat, the knife lay, still wrapped in the blood-soaked cloth. In the darkness, I couldn't even tell whether or not it had stained the seat, but, seeing a straight stretch of road before me, I grabbed the bundle and stuffed it into the glove compartment. I'd have to clear up any mess later on. There was no time right now. Close-up hits always took it out of me; it was much simpler to kill from a distance, with a gun. But my last hit, just ten minutes ago, had become unexpectedly complicated. I ended up having to use the knife; not the way I'd planned it. I hadn't had chance to prepare for the mess. Normally, I'd have had a fresh set of clothes in the car, but not today. That was clumsy, especially given where I had to go next.

I had just four minutes now, and my heart was actually thundering. I had to clear my head or I'd mess the whole thing up. There was so much riding on it; I'd already let the boss down more than once recently. I had to get this one right.

Around me now, the town streaked by. A red light; I ran it. A horn; I gave them the finger and threw the car round a corner. A lorry; I hit the brake hard, bracing my back against the seat as the ABS kicked in and I guided the car between lorry and bus. Several more frantic manoeuvres as I hurtled deeper into the town's sprawl. At last, the tower block. But as I slowed, I saw the familiar black hatchback pulling into the block's private car park ahead of me. It was him. Slipping lower in my seat, I sped past the entrance and round the next corner. Christ, what was I going to do now? I had to get up to the flat before him. That was the plan. It had all been worked out so carefully.

The tyres squealed as I turned another corner, and brought the car to a halt behind the flats. Double yellows; it didn't matter.

I almost dropped the key as I switched off the ignition and flung open the door. I had to compose myself. This was ridiculous! I was practically panicking. I grabbed the package from the back seat, and the crow bar, and hurried towards the tall building, the package tucked under my jacket to keep it out of the rain. I knew I couldn't use the front door; I'd blow the whole thing if I was spotted now. So I scaled the wire fence and hurried round the side of the tower block.

With a few frantic jerks on the crowbar, I forced open the fire exit and hurried inside. I flung the crowbar into the dark space beneath the stairs and I could still hear the ringing of metal on concrete when I reached the second floor. I paused for breath, remembering a time when I'd have climbed a tower block stairwell without breaking a sweat. Thank God I was only heading for the fourth floor.

When at last I arrived, I was gasping for air, but I didn't have time to recover. I eased open the fire door and peered into the space beyond, where the two heavily graffitied lift doors stood side by side. I heard the soft chime which told me one lift was arriving, and without any further hesitation I slipped past and round the corner. Behind me, the lift wheezed open, and voices spilled out. I ran the length of the corridor, fumbling in my pocket for the key the boss had given me yesterday along with the words, "Let me down again and I'll kill you." I managed to slip it in the lock, glancing behind me at the corner I'd just come round. The corridor was still empty, but would only be so for another second or two.

I suddenly remembered to give the four-beat knock, just in case; then, I pushed the door open and slipped into the darkness of the flat, clicking it shut behind me.

"It's me," I hissed into the gloom. "Stay down."

"Bloody 'ell, Mike," came a voice. I couldn't see him but I knew it was Tim, my oldest friend. We'd served in the Middle East together, seen plenty of action there. "Cuttin' it a bit fine aren't you? We saw 'em pull up!"

"Shut up," I said. "They're right behind me."

I made straight for the pale glow of the kitchen area, slamming my shin into the unseen corner of a coffee table and sending something flying.

I limped round the end of the counter which partially divided the lounge from the kitchen, and dropped to the floor, desperately trying to control my breathing. There was someone else nearby, but I couldn't see who. I heard a few quiet voices and a snigger. I shushed them crossly.

I heard the door open. I removed the package from inside my jacket and put it on the floor beside me. The light came on and I heard his voice, his high, rippling giggle.

And this was the moment I'd come for. It seemed to happen so slowly: I stood, revealing my presence, and gazed at my little boy. He was looking down at the photos I'd knocked off the coffee table, but his mother's hard, brown eyes were pointing straight at me. And then the room was full of people, appearing from behind the sofa, from the curtains, the bathroom, the kitchen.

"Surprise!" They cacophonied.

David was stunned into silence for a moment, then his gorgeous smile sprang into life as his aunts, uncles, cousins and friends laughed and clapped and all spoke at once.

And he saw me.

"Dad!" I laughed and moved towards him with my arms wide, and everyone seemed to part for us. He threw himself into my embrace and I whirled him round with delighted enthusiasm. I kissed him and cried out, "Happy birthday, son!" I sat him on the counter top and handed him his present. I hadn't even had time to get wrapping paper for it; it was still in the packaging it had arrived in. "Here you go," I said. "Sorry I haven't wrapped it." He smiled and tore into it. I looked past him at his mother. She couldn't fault me this time. I'd made it, just as we'd arranged. But even so, she was standing there, arms folded, giving me that 'I hate you' look, and now the room was full of excited people who didn't quite know whether or not it was alright to speak.

"Hello, Boss," I said. I'd always called her that, even back when things were good between us.

"Don't call me that, Mike," she warned.

David pulled his new football top from the package. "Thanks, Dad," he said.

"That's alright, son," I grinned. "Tell you what," I said, as I took off my jacket and loosened my tie, "work's been going pretty well recently." That was as much for his mother's ears as his. And, if I'm to be honest, everyone else's too. "I'll take you shopping tomorrow, maybe get you that bike you wanted." Behind David, the boss sighed and shook her head. Nothing was ever good enough for her.

"Dad," David said, but I was busy out-glaring the boss, and enjoying the spell we had cast over the rest of the people in the room. "Dad," David said again, but I had just noticed the way Tim had moved across next to her, and she'd given him that warm, welcoming look she used to give me, and everyone seemed to be staring at me. "Dad."

"What?" I said, instantly regretting the note of anger in my voice, but everyone was staring at me and I was starting to feel paranoid, defensive.

"Why's your shirt got that red hand print on it?"

Among the Flotsam

The gentle waves hissed like elegant ball gowns on delicate ladies. It was early.

The tide retreated slowly, its work done, its deliveries made: driftwood from a pirate ship, green kelp freshly selected from Neptune's garden, and a mermaid's mirror. It left them in a neat line halfway up the beach, dividing wet sand from dry.

This part of the beach was deserted, as it always was so early in the morning. Even during the hottest days not many people bothered to venture down here; being away from the main attractions of the funfair and the town centre it was usually quiet and empty, save for the few visitors who craved isolation and peace. Here, the golden sands could remain untouched for days, like virgin snow, and the dust devils and white horses and laughing spirits of the wind could play and dance unnoticed. So it was unlikely that anyone would discover the thing which the sea had mislaid.

The head lay still, propped at a slight angle on the sand as though it were deep in thought. From a distance it looked like a bundle of seaweed, or a discarded bag; no-one would assume it was a head. As the tide retreated, the town was just coming to life.

The funfair too began to live. Music and voices drifted down on the wind which distorted them and tangled them so that, from this lonely place, they were nothing but a gentle babble like a stream tumbling over rocks, and the waves of the sea competed to drown them out.

The head seemed content to just listen.

A crooked man, old as ghosts, walked his dog along the beach. He was always here early, perhaps to beat the hustle and bustle of the day. He walked among the spiky grass of the dunes; the sand was firmer there and easier on ancient legs. But the greying sheep dog, old as she was, trotted happily along the soft sand of the beach, leaving deep paw prints behind her. She would often stop and sniff at something she found, digging like a happy child. As she sniffed, her master would amble on ahead, alone with his memories. The dog would wander far, forgetting herself sometimes, off across the wet sand which the receding waves had revealed; occasionally she would glance up to check on her master for reassurance: the crooked figure atop the dunes, dark today against the deep blue sky. As for the master, he just walked among the spirits of his past; at times his eyes would sparkle suddenly and he would smile to himself, and at other times his eyes would darken and he would shed a silent tear.

Today, as the man reminisced, the dog investigated the beach, following her curiosity, and her curiosity led her to the head. She sniffed, cautiously backed away, stalked it, growled; she crouched, ears back, chest flat to the sand, her swinging tail holding her rump high. It was tricky fixing eye contact with someone whose head was at such an angle but she tried, perhaps thinking it would get up and play if she stared pleadingly for long enough. But no, the head's empty eyes just stared back.

After a minute of confused stalking, a shrill and distant whistle whipped through the air. Seeing that her master was almost out of sight, the dog ran off, disillusioned. As she leapt into a run she scattered dry sand in the head's hair, but it didn't seem to mind. And now it was alone again.

In the hazy distance the fair was becoming lively, music and voices swirled in the summer air and memories were made. People splashed in the sea and laughed - or screamed - together. A little later, as the sun rose high and the pale moon too inched its way into the bright sky, two young people, a man and a woman, walked away from the noise of the fair to find a more secluded spot. They dropped their towels on the dry sand up near the dunes and ran down to splash around in the waves. They swam and bathed; they rolled and clambered over one another and they battled with great swords of water which they carved up from the ocean with a sweep of the arm, and then they scurried back up the beach again, splashing across the dark, wet sand, leaping the ragged band of flotsam, then churning the dry sand with their wet feet. They fell onto their towels and laughed, and as they held each other the distant waves chattered and spied, slowly reclaiming the wet sand. The head just watched.

After a while, the couple bundled their towels together and strode off through the dunes, laughing still, battling as they went. She was on his back as they dipped behind the grassy crest of the dunes but their voices lingered upon the sand long after the couple were gone from view.

The sun was high now, and the waves were clawing their way back up the sand, swirling into the footprints left behind by the beach's guests. Slowly, haltingly, as the hot day drifted by, they crept towards the flotsam until the soft bubbles were licking around the head, caressing it, gently washing away the sand which the dog had kicked across its cheeks and forehead, removing a strand of weed which had been draped across its nose. And then, as the tide rose, it lifted the head, gently, as though careful not to break its reverie, and carried it back out to sea.

In the distance, the big wheel turned.

Eulogy

"Thomas was ..." I begin. "He was ..." The church is crowded with mourners: his daughters, his two ex-wives, old friends, locals. Hats bob; the air is still. I'm already struggling to say the words, and I've only just started. I don't know if I'll make it to the end. "He was my lifelong friend," I manage. "My best friend." I am forcing the words from myself, looking out across the congregation of damp eyes and sorrowful smiles. They are united in their love for him, the rogue that he was. As I blunder my way through the eulogy, I find myself glazing over. My own words stir memories which rise like smoke to sting my eyes and cloud my view.

I had met Thomas on my first day at school. That is more than eighty years ago now. The school was a tiny stone building with just one room. It seemed cathedral-sized to me back then; it's an antiques showroom now. He was rough-and-tumble, I was a cry-baby. I don't know why we put up with each other. According to my mother, Thomas used to steal my toys, and I used to let him. We had a strange relationship, Thomas and I. It was a small village. There weren't many children at all, and we were the only boys our age. We played out together, but, if there had been other boys the same age as us, I wonder if Thomas and I would have bothered with each other.

I'm aware that the church is cold, despite the big heaters whining and wheezing away. I find their noise intrusive and incongruous, but of course I've been coming here all my life, long before the heaters were installed, and now they are as decrepit as I am. I've read a paragraph or two now, and I'm hardly hearing my own words. I thought I'd be able to do it, to keep myself together until the end, and I'm surprised by how much I'm struggling now. And then I get to a sentence which brings the past sharply into my mind. "He was a war hero." That's what I've written, but I know the truth. Only me. He became a war hero, yes, but that wasn't the whole story.

We had the misfortune of being the perfect soldiering age when war broke out. We went off together to fight for our country. Thomas left several broken hearts behind in the village; I left only one, and that was my mother's. I was always the quiet one. Most girls probably didn't even know I existed back then. And I was not tough, not brave. Thomas was. Everyone knew that. I wonder now if my mother ever expected me to return. As it happened, we had a quiet time of it for the first several months of our service, sailing around Africa all the way to the Far East. In fact, I think it was almost six months before we saw any fighting. We were lucky, for that long at least.

But we'd had our fair share of the action by the end of it. It's funny, but we were always together, even though Thomas was a real lad and everyone wanted to get him drunk, or hear him tell a joke or sing a bawdy song, and I was quiet and uncomfortable, never quite sure if people wanted me there or not. In fact, the only time anyone paid me much attention was when Thomas said something disparaging about me, which he did quite a lot, to get a laugh. Yet somehow that put me slightly at my ease, and we stuck together. So, when we were pinned down by enemy fire one day, it was he and I who crawled on our bellies into a bomb crater as the shells and bullets screamed overhead. We rolled to relative safety in the mud, and looked at each other. Neither of us had ever fired our guns in anger by that time, and were both struggling to keep ourselves together. Those two little infants from the village school, how had we ended up here?

And when a Japanese soldier rolled himself over the crater's lip, also seeking cover, none of us knew what to do. The soldier obviously hadn't known the crater was already occupied, and he practically landed on my head. We all suddenly panicked, and scrambled away from each other, but the Jap was clearly more experienced than us, and had his wits about him. His rifle was pointing straight at us before Thomas and I had even remembered which way round ours went. There was a brief, painful, desperate silence between the three of us as the Jap decided which of us to kill first. Then he pointed his rifle at me and pulled his trigger, but the wet weapon didn't fire. As he pulled back the bolt for his second go, a touch of anguish in his narrow eyes, I fumbled ineffectually with my rifle, which I had ended up partially sitting on, and he pulled his trigger again. Still it didn't fire, but he was so fast! He was on me, shoving my rifle so that I fired it into the mud, and his knees were in my gut and his hand at my throat; I fought him but he had me pinned. All I could do was struggle and thrash like when Thomas and I used to wrestle at school - he'd always get the better of me, just like the Jap was now. But suddenly the Jap went rigid, then limp. He fell on me, his neck bleeding into my face. I rolled him off me and turned, breathless and shaking, to thank Thomas, but Thomas was just disappearing over the top of the crater's edge, and his rifle was still there where he'd been sitting. He'd panicked, and left me, and a stray bullet had killed the Jap.

We never, ever talked about that, Thomas and I.

But Thomas pulled himself together and became a war hero. One day he dragged our bleeding and shouting sergeant major from the battlefield. Even as the blood pumped from the stump of the major's severed leg, the cantankerous old sod was still roaring motivational disdain at his men, most of whom had already fled. Thomas dragged him backwards through the mud to safety. It was a brave act, and one which Thomas never stopped bragging about. He'd obviously forgotten about the Jap in the crater. And he never mentioned the brave things he saw me do. No. He was the war hero, not me.

Hail on the windows is competing with the rattling heaters now, and some of the congregation are quietly slipping their coats back on. "He was very well loved ..." I find myself saying. It's true, he was well loved. The fact that this draughty old church is packed to the rafters on a day like today is testament to that. His big, shiny coffin is surrounded by flowers, and no-one seems able to take their eyes off it. How fitting that he should be the centre of attention, even in death. After the war, Thomas was often the centre of attention in the pub, entertaining the old folk and the young girls with exaggerated tales of his own exploits.

I didn't ever really mind that he got all the attention and I was always his straight-man, and sometimes his fall-guy too. He still made jibes about me in front of the girls and the lads he was trying to impress. I'd grown up with that; it didn't hurt or offend me, not in any conscious way at least. In fact, I barely even noticed it. It was my mother who would point it out to me, but we were grown up now, Thomas and I. After the horrors we'd been through together, all I wanted was peace. Besides, we were friends. I knew he was only joking. And by then I had fallen in love with Sylvia, and she had fallen for me, so Thomas could do and say what he wanted. I really didn't care.

I hear my own voice droning on: "... popular with the ladies ..." This draws a knowing titter from some members of the congregation.

There were some girls I'd expected to see right through his act, to see beyond the bravado and jokes, but they didn't; even some of the sharp, clever girls. He could charm anyone.

Even Sylvia.

I couldn't believe she could be so blind, but more than that, I couldn't believe *Thomas* could betray me like that. How could he? He knew I loved her. And yet, the pain it caused me was more to do with *his* betrayal than *hers*. Thomas and I were friends through circumstance; two totally different people who had played together since our earliest days just because there was no-one else to play with, but I suppose I'd been won over by his charms just like everyone else. I was heartbroken, but in the end, I realised that the thought of losing Thomas was worse than the thought of losing Sylvia.

I didn't want to forgive him, but he was like a brother to me. Besides, we were both still living in the village. Our lives were entangled. I swallowed my pride, and my sorrow, and let him back in.

I look up, for a moment, at some of the faces before

17

me. Many of them are people I know, but very few of them are people I know well. I know them through Thomas. I've met them at his parties and gatherings, or at one of his weddings. They are all wearing that strange expression of both grief and fondness merged together, like heavy rain oddly backlit by evening sun. 'He was a successful politician,' I remind them. He was. He had the gift of the gab of course. He talked himself onto the local village council, and his career went from there. He was kind enough to give me a job as an office clerk. I think this was sort of his way of saying sorry for Sylvia, but looking back I can see it was also a way of keeping me in check. I think, deep down inside, he saw me as some kind of competition. Not that I ever competed with him for jobs, or women, or the respect of our friends and neighbours, but somehow he pitted himself against me, and always came out on top. This was something I only realised in much later years, long, long after the death of my wise old mother who had seen through him right from the start.

I worked for Thomas for many years. He knew how to throw a great Christmas party, and got himself voted into local government time and time again. A long and illustrious career he had, and I was there with him, at his heels, the whole time. We both retired after three decades together, during which time he had been married twice, fathered at least six children by at least three different women, and I'd had a lovely marriage of my own. My Margaret. She had seen what Thomas was like. She could see right through him just like my mother had done. The stupid thing was I always found myself defending him to her. She was happy enough to accept him as my friend, but always careful to point it out to me when she felt he had said something cutting, or derogatory. He said such things without even realising it, without meaning it. I never felt there was malice in him. But Margaret would just raise her eyebrows knowingly, as if she didn't believe that I couldn't see it.

It all seems too long ago now. Margaret has gone. My mother went long before she did. And now Thomas has gone too.

There was only one way in which fate was cruel to him; it crippled him with arthritis in his later years. But he'd never given in to it, and I have to say I admired his tenacity. I tried to talk him into getting a stairlift, but he wouldn't hear of it. He was too proud. He wouldn't accept that he could barely walk, let alone get up and down the stairs anymore. Towards the end, I'd pop in several times a day, often bringing him some shopping – there was no way he could get to the shops anymore, and he certainly wasn't going to be seen "pootling about on one of those dreadful old-people's dodgem cars" as he called them. So he relied on me, and one or two others, to do his shopping, vacuuming, washing, and so on. He was often upstairs when I went round though. I was sure he put himself through that torture before I arrived just so I would see that he was able to get up there. I wasn't fooled. I knew each ascent was a painful, exhausting battle for him. I walk with a stick myself now and I find the stairs hard enough without the curse of arthritis. Once or twice he even conceded to let me help him get back down again. It was awful to see how such an agile, lively man had been twisted and withered by this disease. Still, we both agreed, there were worse things in the world. He still had his marbles, and his memories.

But that was his only suffering. He'd lived a charmed life. His daughters loved him, despite his regular dalliances. Even his ex-wives still seemed pretty well-disposed towards him. He was fondly remembered by the community for his political work and his wonderful parties. Sometimes, recently, I have wondered why.

The other day, I was upstairs in his study. I'd delivered his shopping, vacuumed round a bit, and made him some dinner. He never thanked me. He seemed to feel I owed him this, as payment for his friendship, and perhaps for the employment he'd given me in the past. I was his carer now, though I was suffering the slings and arrows of old age myself too. And ... And ... I hadn't mentioned to him my recent diagnosis. Somehow, I imagined he'd think it was right that I should die before him. He was the better man after all. He had always been more important. I'd always been his minion.

It was my diagnosis which changed me. I am dying. I can't complain. I'm into my nineties. I've had decades more good living than many people get. But still, why should he live longer than me?

I look at the congregation before me. They are all here for him. He really was loved. I wonder how many there will be at my funeral. Some of these people probably didn't even know who I was until today. I have no children, no living wife, no fond ex-wives. I haven't done wonderful things for the community. I won't be remembered as a war hero.

But at least I am still here. That is one thing I have over him.

I've stopped reading the eulogy and find myself just

staring across the church at nothing in particular. I am remembering how that evening with Thomas ended. We'd chatted over whisky and chess in his upstairs study. I'd offered to help him to the bathroom but he'd refused. I bade him goodbye then, and left him sitting there.

At the top of the stairs was a radiator, and on the radiator, a large, thick towel. I'd put it there myself, earlier on, after emptying the washing machine for him. I leant on the radiator for extra support as I made my way down the first couple of steps to where the stairs turned a corner. As I did so, I dislodged the towel. I hadn't meant to of course, but as I was about to pick it back up, a thought crossed my mind.

A minute or two later I was at the foot of the stairs, looking up at the fuse box in the hall. It was one of those nice modern ones with trip-switches rather than fuses. It was me who'd arranged for the electrician to come and fit it; the old one had been an accident waiting to happen.

It seems so out of character now, but years and years and years of something I couldn't quite explain had built up inside me without me even knowing it. And I am dying.

I tripped the master switch off and all the lights went out. And I left, almost before I'd heard Thomas calling out to ask why he'd been plunged into darkness.

I made my way home, and I slept very peacefully that night. My mother and Margaret were both in my dreams. They seemed to understand.

In the morning, I let myself into Thomas's house, as I so often did. He was lying at the bottom of the stairs, lifeless. His feet were still partly tangled up in the towel. I popped the master switch back on and the lights sprang needlessly into life. I looked down at him, and felt nothing, although he had been kind to me sometimes; he had been my friend.

I hadn't known for sure that my actions would kill him, but I knew that was what I'd hoped. Now I will die too, slowly, painfully, but at least I won't be leaving him behind to gloat.

I can't finish the eulogy. After a few long moments of my silence, someone steps up and gently guides me back to my seat. Through my fog of memories and tears I can't even tell who it is. Several people try to soothe me with gentle words, and slowly, like the way a steam engine comes to life, a round of applause begins.

Love Hate Relationship

So that's it then is it? You're just going to sit there, as if that's the end of it. As if everything's alright. You're impossible! You won't even have an argument about it! Why can't you just be honest? Why can't you just say, "Sorry, I messed up. It's a perfectly simple task and I've done it a thousand times before, but I've made a stupid mess of it today because I'm in that kind of mood." I mean, what is your problem?

What are you making that stupid noise for? To calm me down? It just makes me more annoyed! Oh for Christ's sake, I've had enough.

I wish control-alt-delete actually *hurt* you. End now, for crying out loud! No I *don't* want to send an error report, I just want to send my fucking email!

Nathaniel's Daughter

Nathaniel knew there was something different about Lucy these days. She was changing. He hated to see it; he hated to admit it to himself, but she was changing, and there was nothing he could do about it. After everything they'd been through. He'd loved her, and nurtured her, given her a perfect life, but she was changing now in a way which he knew he didn't really understand, but it felt so final, so inevitable. He was losing her, and it was breaking his heart.

Lucy wasn't really his daughter, but that was how he'd always thought of her. He'd rescued her, long ago. He'd taken her from the city and brought her to his utopia.

Nathaniel knew how evil the city was because, since his earliest memories, it had engulfed him and his mother, holding them as shivering prisoners in its alleyways and doorways, in the dark days of distant memory. Sometimes, the city had offered them a house, with wood for windows and rats for pets. Those were the happy times, when the rain couldn't reach them and the wind couldn't bite them. But the city was a monster; it would send nightmares to drive them out into the streets again: hoards of wraiths would want the house for themselves; or fire would claim it; or metal beasts would bash it to bits.

That was all in the fog of distant memory. His mother was all but gone now. The last thing she had done for him was to lead him to this quiet patch of forest which had become home to him and Lucy.

There, with fatherly love, he'd shown Lucy the glory of the forest, and made her forget the city; he'd cleansed her. No longer would she crave bright, white, noisy things; things which roared and shouted and flew and drove; things which towered and smoked and loomed and glowed; the spiteful, angry, murderous city. He'd freed her from all that, and made her lovely.

Of course, she hadn't *looked* lovely by then. Or *smelt* it. In fact, by the time Nathaniel had finished purging her of the city's evil, she'd looked horrible: bloodied and filthy, just like Nathaniel's mother that night in the city, so long ago, after the nasty men had finished with her. That was the night Nathaniel and his mother had fled through rain-glazed streets. And that was the night his mother had become strange and white and sparkly, glowing like a moonlit cloud, no longer able to hold him, to kiss his forehead or grip his hand or tell him a story. From that night onwards, she was always almost out of sight, just disappearing around the next corner, or peering at him from behind a post box. And sometimes she wasn't there at all. Nathaniel, aching into himself, wondered what he had done wrong.

After that, time seemed to have broken into bits. Sometimes, the past and the present were far apart, and sometimes close together, and sometimes the wrong way round. That was when Nathaniel was lost and alone. It was when he hid from people; when he was a shadow in the bushes and the bins. His mother seemed to come and go in those days, as if she didn't know how to stay in the world and kept slipping out of it. But he would glimpse her sometimes, and he'd follow her. Why would she not come to him? Did she not want him anymore? Sometimes he'd hear her sobbing, just around a corner, or she'd suddenly whisper in his ear and make him jump, but when he turned she was only a distant glow. He followed her but could never catch her up. And a great pain of love and loss grew like a stone in his heart.

It was in those strange, jumbled days that he followed her, slowly – street by street, district by district, day by day and week by week – out of the city. Her magic, white glow freed him at last from the city's grip. On bloodied, bare feet, he followed her forever and forever, until there was a forest around him. It was a paradise, and he loved it. He whirled and laughed, and threw handfuls of leaves all over himself. He made the forest his home, and explored its depths; he talked to the birds and ate fruit and roots and rabbits.

But soon – or perhaps not soon at all, he couldn't tell – his mother was hardly there, fading like summer. Her crying, her whisper, her glow grew faint and distant. He felt her watching him, but knew she was leaving him. Who would love him now?

"You're a big boy, Nathaniel," she whispered to him one night, perhaps in a dream. "You are full of love." When he woke, her words blew about inside his head like wind-swept moths. He knew what he needed to do. He knew why his mother had brought him here.

So, he sneaked back to the edge of the forest, from where he could see into parks and gardens. He saw nasty, city-wraiths, like the men who had come and made his mother change on that horrible night. And he saw their children.

Lucy was beautiful. So young and smooth and clean, and her laughter was like his mother's. It made the stone in his chest pulse and ache to see her, to know that she was part of the city, to know it would absorb her soon, and make her horrid. So he'd rescued her.

He'd taken her deep into the forest, away from houses and roads and the stink of the city, to a pretty cleft in a wooded hillside he had found. There she could be cleansed. Lucy had struggled to understand at first. She had fought Nathaniel. She'd begged him to take her back to the wraiths and the stink from whence she'd come, but he wouldn't. And, as each little devil was beaten from her, she'd resisted, desperate to hold onto them, to let them posses her. Nathaniel had not realised how much in the grip of the city she already was. He had to thrash and command and wring the devils from her until he could barely breathe, and he collapsed from exhaustion, utterly spent.

But he had done it. The evil had gone, and she had calmed. At last, the birds could start returning to the branches from which her screams had driven them, and peace returned to this tiny, wooded valley.

When the evil had gone from Lucy, Nathaniel had cleaned her up with water from the stream, washed the mud and blood and vomit from her hair and clothes and soft, pink skin, and made her pretty again. He could see that pleased her. Then, he'd sat her on a chair which a family of gypsies had recently dumped in a nearby ditch. He'd mended it, and now it was a throne for the good princess Lucy.

Sometimes, Nathaniel thought that was years and years ago, and sometimes he was sure that it was only yesterday, and sometimes he wondered if it had ever really happened at all, if his mother had ever happened, if there had ever been anything else in the world but him and Lucy living happily together here, in the forest.

Nathaniel told Lucy the tales his mother had told him, and Lucy listened like a good girl as the autumn leaves fell onto her jet-black curls, and the rain dripped, and a congregation of deer and rabbits gathered all around, and a choir of sparrows, starlings and robins sang beneath waterfalls of golden sunlight which gushed from the vaulted rafters of the forest canopy.

But Lucy was changing now. He hated that. Just when everything was perfect. Why? Why had her skin lost that happy glow; why was that innocent radiance gone from her eyes? Why, when Nathaniel stroked her skin, did she feel like a stone, hard and icy? And when he ran his rough and heavy hands over her once silken locks, why did some of it come away in his fingers, like cobwebs?

Fly

"You have to go now," I say, because the sight of him in my bed is making me want to screw up my eyes and say the word "safe" four times and one for luck. I resist because he's looking up at me now. I'm standing next to the bed, with a towel round my body. I've already showered last night off me. He grins. He wants me to come back to bed with him but I say it again, to show him I mean it.

"Well, that's me told," he says sarcastically, throwing back the covers and huffing through his nose. I can't believe I felt so different last night. It's always the same. The night is exciting and passionate, sexy and coke-fuelled. The morning is horrible and dark and I feel wrong. Why do I do it? A fly brushes close to my face and I waft at it, then I turn away because now I have to screw my eyes up so tight they hurt and the black world behind my lids is filled with blotches of colour. Safe safe safe safe. And one for luck: safe.

I walk out of the bedroom. "Livvy," he calls after me, quite gently. I'm shamed that he remembers my name. I can't remember his. He knows nothing else about me though. He doesn't know I'm a fucking weirdo. I can hide it for a while, like when I'm out with my friends and I've had a couple of glasses of wine, like last night in the club. When he came over, I couldn't look at him at first, but he thought that was because I'm shy. That's what they always think. Boys seem to like that. I'm not shy though. It's just that sometimes I can't look at people because I'm afraid my eyes can hurt them, like give them cancer or something.

I scrunch my eyes up really tight again until the blotches come, to get rid of that horrible word, and then I go downstairs. Safe safe safe safe. Safe. The filth in the house makes me feel sick. There are just too many out-of-reach corners and surfaces in a big old place like this. That bloody fly seems to be following me. I hate flies, but they are always too quick to kill so I end up putting up with them.

While no-one's around, I take the opportunity to open my mouth really wide until it stretches at the sides and feels as if it's going to tear and I can hear that rushing in my ears like when you yawn. I've been needing to do that for ages.

God, why can't I just be normal? I know I don't *need* to do these things. I know my eyes *can't* give people cancer and I know the house isn't filthy. But even though I *know* all that, I *feel* the opposite. And my feelings are stronger than my knowing. I can't stop myself. As I reach the kitchen, I even have to do the one where I stretch my arms, legs and neck so that all my joints burn and I'm standing on tip-toe until my body feels cleansed. Then I relax, worried that he might have followed me downstairs and seen me doing that. I turn; he hasn't. The cleansed feeling will only last for a few minutes and I'll have to do it all over again. I can tell it's going to be like that today. Probably because of what I did last night, on some sort of deep, psychological level that I've never managed to unpick.

I put the kettle on and stand in the middle of the kitchen with my arms folded and shoulders hunched up. I can't quite bear to touch anything unless I have to. In my head, I'm re-living last night, in disjointed, non-chronological chunks: the sex, mostly, but also laughing in the pub with Lisa and Hannah. God knows what happened to them. I do manage to have a laugh sometimes, after a bit of self-medication. Sometimes I manage to forget the weird thoughts and obsessions which fill my head, and just get on and have a laugh, like normal people.

I see that fly sitting on the work-top. It must have found a crumb or something. I try not to think about its horrible mouth-parts, but I already know from my GCSE days that they are like enormous red lips on the end of a trunk-like tube, with grooves all the way up inside, lined with little serrated teeth, and as I watch they are puking bile onto the crumb and sucking it up as the crumb is reduced to a bubbling froth by the bile. They vomit in reverse: their bile digests the food before they eat it, then, when it's all turned to sick, they suck it back up, relishing the taste of their own pre-digested dinner. It makes me want to shriek. I look around for a way to kill it. I grab a tea-towel and take a swipe. The towel slaps the work-top but the fly escapes, and settles on the ceiling, looking down at me triumphantly. And now the tea-towel has got fly-puke-dinner on it so I'll have to boil-wash it. In fact, I might never be able to bring myself to use it again. I might as well just keep it as a fly swat now. Safe safe safe safe. Safe. Eyes-scrunch. Mouth-stretch.

The kettle clicks off, the water bubbling inside it like fly-bile on a crumb, and footsteps on the stairs make me

31

turn my head. "Great place," he says. "I hardly noticed it last night!" The place is actually pretty odd: an old chapel with lots of open-plan space and a mezzanine floor. Very modern, in an ironic sort of way. In fact, the ironic thing is it was modernised in the early 90s and it's all looking a bit shabby now. He's only wearing his boxers, and he's breathing his breath into the air I have to breathe. He's grinning laconically, as if we have a shared appreciation for last night's naughtiness, and I am suddenly frozen by the thought that he might try to kiss me. He's coming towards me, swaggering as if he's proud of what he achieved last night, and then the cat-flap clatters and in comes that little tabby cat that seems to think it lives here. I can barely bring myself to touch it, but it gives me a chance to duck away from the encroaching kiss, and I grab the cat, turn it round and shove it straight back out of the flap. I move the bin in front of it so the cat can't get back in. I feel guilty now, because sometimes I welcome the creature in, and let it sit on my lap while I watch Hollyoaks. I even stroke it sometimes. But I can't do that today.

Now I've got cat-lick all over my hands, so I push past the human intruder and run the hot tap. Over my shoulder I say, "I have to go out soon, so you'll have to go. I've got to get ready." But he comes right up behind me and puts his hands on my waist. He dips his head towards my neck, moving my hair out of the way with his stubbly chin. All I can think about is his skin-cells detaching themselves from his face and losing themselves in my wet hair. I don't care that the towel I've got around me isn't long enough to cover my cellulite, and his hands are on the fat around my hips. I just care about the air coming out of his lungs, through that mouth and round those teeth that haven't been cleaned, and the skin-cells he's shedding onto me. I've got cat-lick on my hands and I'm about to have his dirty mouth on my neck and I want to swat him away with the tea-towel. I twist so he can't quite reach me with his lips, and I start to wash my hands, even though the water isn't properly hot yet. The water has to be scolding hot, otherwise it won't kill the germs. He thinks I'm joking though. He can't believe I can be acting like this when I was so into him last night, but he doesn't know me. I am fickle in the extreme. I'm scrubbing my hands and he's trying to kiss my neck and I'm twisting away from him and I'm scrubbing hard even though the bloody water refuses to heat up and he refuses to give up until I elbow him sharply in the ribs. He gasps and backs right off.

"What the fuck?" he says. "What was that for?" Still rubbing my hands together, the water finally getting hot and painful, I say to him, "Like I said, I've got to go. Sorry."

"Christ, what did I do?" he says as I scrub. He's still standing there and I can smell his morning breath, and I see it in the air like a yellow gas and I hold my breath for as long as I can. Finally, only breathing out, not in, I manage to say, "Nothing. It's just me." I dry my hands on the towel I'm wearing, and walk out of range of his breathing. I open a window, then think about the fly and imagine others coming in to join it. Why is it that flies are only ever capable of flying *in* through a window, not out? I close it again, and hold my breath. I feel as if I'm going to scream at him if he doesn't go, and I wish to God I could remember his name, but I can't. I'm desperate to do the eye-scrunch mouth-stretch thing, and I'm saying safe safe safe safe under my breath, but I can't do any of it properly because he's looking at me. He has very pretty, dark eyes. If I wasn't trapped in this OCD bubble I'd find him very attractive. I did last night. But he's started to tell I'm a bit mental and he seems reluctant to delve. At least he's realised we're probably not going back to bed today. Maybe he'll go now. Funny, I'd thought he was kind. He does look it. Thank goodness he isn't. The kind ones always want to make me look at them in the morning even though I can't, and think they can make me feel better by saying something gentle. They think I'm being shy and embarrassed, when what I'm really thinking is I wish they'd fuck off out of my house. This one though, he seems to realise he's not wanted, and he doesn't seem to care that much. He got what he came for, and now he's going.

He smiles one last wry and cheeky smile, then heads back upstairs. I take in a very long breath. I notice the cat is sitting on the windowsill now, looking into the kitchen. I've not lived here long, and I think the lady who lived here before me used to feed it. I wonder if the cat even realises I'm not her. Last week it brought a dead mouse in! It left it by the front door. I was having one of my bad days and when I saw the mouse I couldn't bring myself to go near it. All I could think about was rodent-juice seeping from its decaying flesh and running into the gullies between the tiles, and rodent-gas rising into the air. I ended up having to knock on my neighbour's door for help. Mortifying.

Safe safe safe safe. Safe.

That bloody fly is driving me mad. It's dive-bombed

my head several times as if it's *trying* to piss me off. I'm going to have to kill it. I lash out with the tea-towel, slapping several surfaces in quick succession as it darts from place to place, but it's like they move in a different time-zone to us. No matter how quickly I whip the towel through the air, it sees it coming and casually side-steps it. I wish I wasn't so mental. I wish I wasn't so paranoid about using fly-spray, but if I release some of that stuff into the air I'll be breathing it in. How do I know it won't give me cancer (safe safe safe safe, eye-scrunch, mouth-stretch) or some sort of hideously debilitating nerve disease (safe safe safe safe, eye-scrunch, mouth-stretch)?

So the fly lives and I feel a rage rising inside me. "Get out of my house, you fucking little shit!" I yell so violently that it scrapes my throat.

"Alright, alright, I'm going," comes the irritated reply as the boy-with-no-name comes down stairs pulling on his T-shirt. I should tell him I didn't mean him, but instead I just storm past him as if we've had a row and I'm not speaking to him. I know I'm being ridiculous, and totally unfair, but he has to go. His presence is making me want to cry. I can feel him looking at me as I head upstairs. He must be completely confused, but at least he'll have something to laugh about with his mates.

Upstairs, I pace, waiting for him to go. I need to clean the house. I need to wash the bed sheets and all of my clothes, even the ones I haven't worn. I need to scrub the bathroom and hoover the carpets. I can't start while he's here because that would defeat the object, so I stand there staring at my bed with its pile of duvet spilling onto the floor, and the used condom leaking onto the rug like a rotting rat.

That fucking fly. It's followed me upstairs! I can't believe it. It flies round my head and lands on the bed-side table. I haven't brought the tea-towel with me. What can I kill it with? I look for my slippers. I find one, and stalk, very slowly, very carefully up to the fly, raising my arm so gently that it'll never suspect what's coming, but it flies off before I've even begun to bring the slipper down! I swipe and slash the air uselessly and stupidly and the horrible little creature buzzes away. But I'm not giving up. Quickly, I grab the pillow that's had his head on it, pull the case off, and now I have a better weapon. The fly lands on the curtain. It's not inside one of the folds, it's right on the outside of one, quite near the bottom. I have a plan. I used to be great at stinging the other girls with the very end of my towel in the changing rooms at school. If you get it just right, it acts like a whip, the tip of it going so fast it can bring up a red welt on a naked thigh. Just think what it could do to a fly! I control my breathing as I line up the pillow case. I'll have only one shot at this. I try to clear my head and relax. I do it!

The pillowcase snaps at the fly; the curtain recoils; the fly drops to the floor. I am victorious!

But, I can't bring myself to touch it. I crouch down, which is quite hard to do when you are wrapped as tight as I am in a bath towel, and look at it. Is it dead? I get up and look for something to scoop it up with. It has to be something I don't want, or won't ever need to touch again. I look at the photos blue-tacked around the outside of my mirror. They'd be perfect, but they are all of people I care about. I couldn't use one of them to scoop a fly up with! I glance back to make sure it's still there. I can't see it at first, so I go back over to where I know it is.

The fucking little fucker's gone! I must have just stunned it. I look around all over the place but I can't see it. I grab the pillow case, making sure I'm not touching the end that hit the fly. I'm like a hunter now. There's no way that thing is going to escape. If I have to tear the house apart I'll find it. The crazy thing is, that isn't a joke. I have to find it now. I am obsessed.

I hear a noise downstairs. What's he doing? Hasn't he gone yet? Out on the small, mezzanine landing, I peer over the banister. I can't see him, but I can hear him in the kitchen, running the tap. He must be getting a drink. God, if someone had yelled "Get out of my house, you fucking little shit!" at me, I wouldn't be hanging around to get a drink. I clench every muscle in my body now, and try to make every joint hurt. I thump my own head repeatedly, until stars splatter my vision. I know this is mental, but I can't help it. Why won't he go?

I turn to go back into my bedroom, and I see the fly. At least, I think it's the same one. I can't even bring myself to entertain the possibility that there's another one. It's on the window, a very tall, wide window that almost runs the full height of the house. There's a gap between the mezzanine and the wall, and the window is sunk into the thickness of the wall, which makes it bloody hard to clean because I can hardly reach it and cobwebs often gather under its arched top. I literally have to risk life and limb if I want to reach those, standing on the metal banister looking down through the gap between the mezzanine and the window at the tiles on the hall floor way beneath me. I do it though, because I am that mental. It's alright if I remember that if I'm going to fall, fall backwards, not forwards.

37

Some of the window's glass panes are coloured. The fly has landed on a little blue one. I think about going and fetching the chair from my bedroom but I hardly dare take my eyes off the fly.

Safe safe safe safe. Safe. I do the mouth-stretch until it feels as if my jaw is going to break.

I think I've stunned the fly, but if I slap it with the pillowcase its foul guts will spread themselves all over the window. The thought literally makes me gag. But if I'm clever, I can get it without making any mess. As quick as I can, I make a hurried journey back into the bedroom and return with a tall beaker of water that I'd fetched at some point last night. I tip what's left of the water into a nearby pot-plant. I know that the fly is stunned. It's used its last reserves of energy to get up as high as it can, and that's where it wants to stay. I hitch up the towel I'm wearing and clamber onto the banister, steadying myself against the wall. Behind me is the landing and in front of me is the window. Between me and the window is the drop. I know how ridiculous it is that I'm more scared of cobwebs and dead flies than I am of a twenty foot drop onto stone tiles, but that's the way I am. Below me, I can just see him now, the boy-with-no-name, just his shoulder and elbow and the side of his head. He's putting his shoes on I think. He doesn't know I'm right above him. I look ahead of me at the fly. Its wings move, but only slightly. It isn't very well. Really slowly, leaning across the gap with one hand on the cold stone wall, I reach forward with the glass.

I hear the front door open. Thank God. He's finally going. But then I hear, "Hello, cat." He says something else that I don't catch, and seems to laugh. And the door slams behind him. Through the window's rippled glass, I can see him walking down the path, and out the gate. I know he's let the cat in, but at least I haven't cleaned the house yet, and a cat is much easier to get rid of than a fly, so I put that out of my mind.

The beaker is hovering towards the drowsy fly. My arm is stretched as far as it can go and I realise I can't reach it. The only thing I can do is sidestep along the banister, like a tightrope-walker. I can't reach the wall anymore. This is dangerous, and stupid. And *mental.* But I'm really not thinking straight.

Now the fly is right in front of me. Again, I reach forward with the glass, aware that if I leave it any longer, the fly will recover from its concussion, and fly off. The window is just a little more than arm's length away. Wobbling, I lean forward, over the gap. I will not be beaten.

I fall forwards. The beaker hits the window pane, sliding slightly sideways with a horrible screech, and I find I am a bridge: my feet on the banister rail, my body across the gap, and all my weight pressing hard against the beaker in my hand which in turn is pressing against the little blue glass pane. And trapped inside the beaker is the fly! I would laugh but I'm busy flailing my free hand around desperate to find something to grab onto. I can't reach the wall. There's no way I can hold this gravity-defying position for long. I never was much good at gymnastics. I adjust my feet, curling my toes to brace them against the sharp edge of the metal banister. My whole body is beginning to shake. My free hand can't find anything to hold onto so ends up on the beaker with my other hand, all my weight pressing into the beaker and into the window. What the hell am I going to do now? I've got the fly. There's no way I'm going to let it get away. And then I realise three things, all at the same time: 1) I've got nothing to slide under the beaker. How could I be so stupid? As soon as I remove the beaker the fly will escape. 2) The cat has come up the stairs and is sitting on the landing, just out of my field of vision. I can feel it watching me. 3) This window, the one almost all of my bodyweight is currently pressing against, is not going to hold. It is made of lots of little panes held together by lead, and thin struts of wood. It's one big sheet of flimsily connected squares and rectangles of glass. I can hear the wood splitting, and can see the lead joins bending outwards.

And then I notice something on the tiles beneath me that wasn't there a few moments ago. I stare at it, trying to bring the dark shape into focus. Oh my God. Is that what I think it is? The cat has left me a present: the most enormous rat I have ever seen in my whole life. It's laid across several tiles, on its side, its tail curled round and its red eye open. And there is blood coming out of its mouth, and guts hanging out of its stomach.

My head spins.

The cat sits on the landing, watching me, as if waiting for my delight at this wonderful present.

The window creaks, and a popping noise comes from one of the wooden struts.

Safe safe safe safe. Safe safe safe safe. But I'm not safe. No matter how many times I say it. I have to get down from here, but I can't. I can't bring myself to release the fly. Even if I could, straightening myself up will mean pushing hard against the window. It will break, and I will go diving forwards through it. I already feel as if I am mid-dive. The only thing I can possibly do is to let myself drop straight down. Right now. Right this second. This is how mental I am: it isn't the drop that worries me, it's what I'll be landing on. The rat just lies there, obliviously rotting its way into my lungs and eyes and hair even from this distance. Horror prickles its way up my body, bores its way into my mind and no amount of eye-scrunching and mouth-stretching can stop it.

I have left it too long. I have prevaricated myself into a very nasty dead end. As the window explodes outwards and I find myself plunging forwards, I see the fly seizing its moment.

I fall. The fly flies free.

The Trouble With Hiring A Hitman

It wasn't even mid-morning yet and Michael already had his fingers tight around the neck of a bottle of Sol, minus the slice of lime. The house which, less than a decade ago, he'd paid others to build for him with his hard-earned solicitor's salary, was silent today. It was always silent now. Always would be.

He'd barely moved for God knew how long, and was beginning to feel as if his body had disappeared, as if his spirit had become part of the air around him. Through the huge expanse of glass which was the kitchen's end wall, he gazed emptily at the garden, the climbing frame he would never bring himself to remove, and the sun lounger beside the unused pool.

It was the deep chime of the doorbell which reminded him where he was. He took a sip of beer and wished it was something stronger. It wasn't until the third chime that he bothered to turn.

He didn't hurry; whoever was at the door, no matter how friendly the face or caring their sentiment, would only serve to remind him of his own wretchedness, his loss, and the dark evil which stirred within him. But the chimes grew longer and quicker, as if the doorbell itself was shouting at him. This was not the postman.

A long gulp of beer gave him strength and he unlocked the door. He pulled it open, almost certain he knew now who would be standing there.

But this wasn't who he'd expected. This was not the fat guy from the Queen's Arms. "Who are you?" he said at last to the heavily bearded, middle-aged man in the cheap blue suit and battered brogues.

"You must be Michael," the man said, and looked him up and down. "You're smaller than I expected," he added, the smoky timbre of his voice glazed with Glaswegian. He glanced behind him at the van he'd parked in the broad and elegant driveway, and then smiled expectantly at Michael. He had a prominent, almost theatrically large nose, an earring, and peppery hair tied back in a loose ponytail. Michael had never seen him before, and wondered how to make him go away. Whoever this man was, Michael had more important things to worry about today. "I'm Keith," said the Scott.

It took Michael a moment to digest that. Then: "Keith? Christ. What are you doing here? Is it done?"

"You'd better let me in," Keith said, softly spoken and level, like a lioness, and he stroked his greying orange beard. Michael stepped back and the man entered, an old canvas holdall swinging at his side.

"Is it *done*?" Michael snapped with Eton-refined brusqueness.

"There's a problem," Keith said. Michael took this like a kick in the stomach. He wanted to scream at the man, he wanted to roar. He felt his molars grinding together so hard it seemed he would push them back into the jaw bone which held them. But, uncharacteristically, he held his frustration back. Although they'd never met, Michael already knew that despite the Scotsman's soft, warm tones, he was deeply, shamelessly, fearlessly violent.

"What has happened?" Michael managed to rein in his bubbling fury just enough to get the question out without his voice crackling.

Keith strode past him, further into the house. "There's been a complication," he said, and drifted into the dining room with almost feminine poise. Michael gulped the last of his Sol, swore under his breath, and followed.

"Sit down," Keith said. Michael looked at him askance. In his own house! "Sit down, Michael," the man said again, beckoning towards one of the dining room chairs. Michael felt compelled to obey. Only then did he notice the huge kitchen knife Keith had already placed on the table, just out of Michael's reach. "I'm going to tie you up now," Keith said.

"*Tie me up?*" Michael went to stand, slamming his empty bottle onto the glass table top, but Keith placed his bejewelled hand against Michael's chest and gently pressed him back into the chair. Keith then crouched and opened his holdall, his back to Michael, the kitchen knife only a couple of feet away. Keith was flaunting his fearlessness, taunting Michael with temptation. For those few seconds, a battle raged inside Michael: he was fairly fit for his age, a strong swimmer, scrum-half shoulders, could still hold his own on the squash court. Keith looked to be twenty or more years older than him, though the loose fitting suit made it hard to judge how fit he was, and Michael knew there were boundaries his own mind would not let him cross, boundaries which were nothing to this man. Michael watched him rummage. He could grab the knife, and plunge it into the man's back, right where his greasy ponytail hung. He could, he *should* ... But they both knew he wouldn't. From his case, Keith lifted out a coil of nylon rope. As he looped it round Michael's body, legs and arms, Michael spat angry questions at him: "Why? What the hell are you doing? Don't you want your money? What about that little shit? Is he dead?" But he didn't dare lift a finger in resistance, and soon the rope was tight, binding him firmly onto the wooden chair, and he gazed up at Keith in utter confusion and boiling rage.

"I'm going to get something from the car," Keith said, looking down at Michael as if he were a sculpture he'd just completed, but was a bit disappointed with. Then he turned and left. Michael felt his hot face cooled by a swarm of autumnal air as the front door opened. He stared at the knife, still sitting there on the tabletop. There was no way he could reach it now. Suddenly, he knew his only hope was to force his way out of the ropes, and he heaved and pulled, unperturbed by the sensation of burning skin. He'd rip his skin off, break his wrists and hands to get out of these bonds ... But Keith clearly knew how to bind a man, and Michael was well and truly bound.

The front door clicked shut and the visitor returned. There was another man with him. Keith was leading him like a pet. This man was wrapped in thick duct tape which held his arms across his chest as if he were in a straight jacket. The tape was wound all around his legs so he had to move in little shuffling hops. It was round his mouth and eyes too. Hunched and trembling, this was a broken man.

"Here, gentlemen, is the problem," Keith said. Carefully, he found a corner of the sticky tape and tore it off the man's face, taking eyebrows, possibly even skin with it. The man yelped, but his red face was revealed.

Michael suddenly struggled again. "What the fuck have you brought him here for?" he spat. "You were supposed to kill him!"

The man – young, handsome, but hard-looking and unhealthy – stared at him.

"Come on, Jake," Keith said to his captive, guiding him towards one of the dining room chairs. "Let's sit you down." He spoke with a carer's bed-side manner. He retrieved more rope from the holdall and soon had the young man tethered as tightly as Michael was. "Christ!" the young man whimpered. "Jesus!" he gasped. "Look, I'll do anything! You don't need to do this!"

"Gentlemen," Keith said, straightening. "Calm down. Let me explain." He looked at them both, almost affectionately, and slid his hand over his ponytail. "You have presented me with a dilemma. Last week, you, Michael, handed a wee envelope to a gentleman acquaintance of mine in the Queen's Arms. That envelope was delivered to me within an hour. By total coincidence, at almost exactly the same time, another envelope was delivered to another acquaintance of mine in the King's Head, and that too was delivered to me with equal haste." Michael could see where this was going. And he was hating this man, with his pretend niceties, his pretend posh suit, his pretend airs and graces. "You'll never guess what," Keith said. He waited, as if for an answer. None came, so he continued, slowly, as if addressing a class of very stupid students. "Inside one envelope was a down-payment and a photograph. It was a photograph of *you*, Jake. And in the other was a down-payment and a photo of *you*, Michael." He paused. "Do you see my problem?" Neither captive knew how to respond, so, in mock exasperation, Keith continued: "Michael, you had hired me to kill a man. That man ... was *this* man. Young Jake here. And Jake? You had hired me to kill Michael. What an incredible coincidence! But the problem is, if I kill one of you, I only get paid by one of you. And if I kill both of you, I get paid by neither of you. Now, I could just get on and kill one of you and be happy to receive the payment from the other; put my losses down to experience. But I'm a passionate man. Once I get the whiff of money, once I smell the prize, I'm afraid, gentlemen, my heart becomes set on winning it. I won't be happy until I receive my payment in full, from both of you, which can't happen of course, so one of you will have to pay me the full amount owed by the pair of you, and the other, well ..."

The room was full of a dark and weighty silence. At last, it was Jake who broke it. "N- n- no! I've got money! I'll pay you! Fuck, don't kill me!"

Keith stood back and looked down at the pair of them, his face darkening. Michael was too busy fighting back rising bile and vomit to be able to counter Jake's efforts, and he stared at the Scotsman, his body cold, inert.

"The trouble with hiring a hitman," Keith informed them, wisely, "is you never know how things are going to pan out. And once you're in, there's no going back." Then he brightened again. "Tell you what," he said, "I'll go and make some coffee. I'll bet you've got one of those percolators that make you wish you had a degree in astrophysics, Michael? I may be a while." With that, he left, and Michael and Jake looked at each other. Jake was young and skinny, his face sallow and drawn from smoking too young. His eyes were big and grey and wet, and Michael felt a flash of pity for him. Pity, but not compassion. He could not feel compassion for this man.

Those grey eyes were scanning him too, sizing him up, trying to work out how to play this vile game, searching for weakness, or desperately trying to read Michael's next move.

"I've got money," Michael told Jake. "Look around you. Is this the house of someone who doesn't have money?" He wasn't sure where he was going with this, but he felt he had the upper hand here. Jake was not much more than a boy. A chav from the estate in town. A junkie and a dealer, yes, but small-time. Surely he couldn't afford the pay-off Keith wanted. Jake just stared, his head giving barely perceptible twitches. The poor boy had no way out. Michael shouted into the kitchen, "I have money, Keith. I'll pay you what you want."

"I have money too!" Jake's panicky vibrato chimed. "You know I have, Keith! I've got lots of money! All stashed away! I can pay you!"

Keith didn't reply. Michael could hear cupboards opening and closing, the fridge door, caught a whiff of that ancient cheese; crockery chinked against crockery.

"Keep talking, boys," Keith called back. "I was right about this percolator. Too complicated for me! I'm going to have to make instant I'm afraid."

"He's going to kill us both," Michael began, quietly, to Jake. He felt himself blink heavily, one eye screwing up involuntarily as sweat seeped into it. Shit. He hadn't wanted Jake to see his panic. But he was panicking. The boy said he had money! He must be lying. But what if he was telling the truth? Christ, Michael thought. What do I do?

"He's going to kill *you*," Jake hissed. "Not me. I can pay him."

"I can pay him too." Michael forced the words out through clenched teeth and dry lips. "I'll double your money!" he called to Keith.

"I'll triple it!" Jake shouted.

There was silence. Michael could feel his hair flopping across his eyes and try as he might he could not shake it away. He knew his composure was gone. Jake could see he was crumbling. But this boy ... surely he couldn't have all the money he claimed to have?

Michael heard the kettle reaching boiling point.

"Sorry?" Keith called to them. "I didn't quite catch that."

"Look," Michael said. He needed to get the boy to talk actual figures. He could go on all day claiming to be able to double and triple the payment, but if Jake knew how much money was actually involved, the evidence would be on his face if he was lying about how much he had. Michael wished he was a poker player. "Do you know how much money you'd need to come up with if you were going to really triple the fee?"

"Twelve grand," Jake muttered into his own chest.

"Twelve grand?" Michael exclaimed triumphantly. The poor lad couldn't even add up! It was more than twice that much! "More like thirty!" Michael announced.

"Thirty?" Jake said, confused.

"Yes. Listen. Five grand each is ten grand–"

"Five grand each? It was two grand wasn't it?"

"Two grand?"

"That's what he charged me. One grand up front. One when it's done."

"What?" Michael said, a new fury rising in him now. Had Keith really only charged Jake two grand to have him killed, but had charged him five grand to kill Jake? He could hear hot water being poured, a teaspoon clattering round inside an expensive earthenware mug.

"Why?" Jake said. "How much did he charge to do me?"

Michael didn't answer. Suddenly, he asked, "Why the hell did you want to have me killed anyway? Do you even know who I am?"

"Yes," Jake said. "I do. You're Eleanor's dad."

Just the very mention of her name enraged him. How dare that little piece of fucking shit even utter her name? Her name should not be anywhere near his poisonous lips. He bucked and writhed, the knife still tantalisingly close on the table top. If he could only get an arm free ...

"Here we are," said Keith, sweeping in and placing a heavy tray of steaming mugs on the table beside the knife. "Do you take sugar?"

"What?" Michael said, a burning, acidic rage purging his fear. "Are you fucking serious?"

"Suit yourself," Keith said, un-rattled. "Jake?"

"No thanks," the boy managed with a little shake of the head.

"Only me then," Keith smiled, and spooned several very large heaped spoonfuls into a mug as his two captives watched in silence. "This is yours, Jake," Keith said, placing one of the mugs on the table edge near to Jake who stared at it longingly. "And yours," Keith said, placing Michael's near to him. Michael looked at him with violent hatred. His dry throat craved that coffee, but his hands were tied and Keith was just taunting his prisoners.

"I think I heard you two discussing figures," Keith said. "Let me explain. Jake, I quoted you two thousand pounds Sterling." His Scottish tongue flicked, snake-like, around the 'r' in 'Sterling'.

"How come—" Michael interrupted, but Keith silenced him with a raised finger.

"You gave me a thousand up front. Michael, I quoted you five thousand pounds Sterling. You gave me two thousand five hundred up-font. So, all we're talking about is the outstanding three and a half thousand. You've made a bold claim, Jake. Can you really triple that? Can you come up with ten thousand five hundred pounds Sterling?"

"Wait," Michael said. "How come you only charged him two thousand?"

Keith eyed him sympathetically. "Please," he said. "Come on, posh boy. Do you really think I'd have any trouble taking you out? I came into your house uninvited earlier on, told you to sit down and you did, and you sat there while I tied you up even though there was a huge knife almost within arm's reach. I'll bet you're kicking yourself now aren't you?" He didn't wait for a response. "Jake, on the other hand, put up quite a battle. He came at me with a flick-knife. He could well have had a gun. Even after I'd hit him on the head with a hammer he kept on fighting me. Oh, and while you, Michael, live in this nice big house with no-one around within earshot, Jake here lives on a crowded estate in a tower-block. I had to get him out, wrapped up in duct-tape, without anyone seeing. It wasn't easy, as you can imagine."

Fleetingly, Michael found himself nodding in agreement with this reasonable assessment, but remembered himself and said, "Fuck you."

"That's very rude. But brave. I think you might be growing some balls, Michael," Keith said, and ruffled Michael's hair. "Now, enough chatter. Which one of you is going to pay me my money? Jake, you've upped the ante to ten and a half thousand. Well, you actually said twelve, but you didn't know the figures, so I'm giving you the benefit of the doubt there. I'm a reasonable man. Any advance?"

"Twenty," Michael said. "I have the money. It's in my account. I can get you it right now."

"Forty!" Jake blurted.

"Forty?" Keith said, twirling a strand of beard. "Jake, I'm not stupid. You haven't got forty thousand pounds to give me, have you. Your tawdry little drugs-ring hasn't made you quite that rich, has it." It was a statement, not a question, and now it was Jake's turn to crumble. He was actually crying now.

"Christ, Keith! Don't kill me! I can change! Please! Please! Christ!"

"Wait," Michael said. "What if I ... What if we withdraw our ..." he floundered around in his head for the right terminology. "What if we withdraw the hits?"

Keith sipped his coffee, and placed the heavy mug on the glass table so slowly and gently it barely made the slightest noise. He actually seemed to be considering this. "Hmmm, I'm listening."

This was an unexpected turn. Could this dangerous man really be prepared to let them both do that? Could they both walk away from this situation?

52

"Well," Michael said, realising this was his chance to talk Keith into the idea. "Well," he said. "Um, we could ... We could forgive each other."

"Yes," Jake said hopefully. "Yes, we could do that!"

"What, so I let you both go?"

"You'd still have your down-payments," Michael said. "You wouldn't have killed anyone, so you wouldn't have to be looking over your shoulder for the rest of your life." *Any more than you already do*, he thought.

To Michael's amazement, Keith nodded, eyebrows raised. "And I let you both go," he said. Michael couldn't believe Keith was actually going to go along with the idea. He felt a hot wave of relief begin to fill his chest. But in the brief absence of his numbing fear, his hatred for Jake returned. Jake was gazing back at him with wide, red eyes, willing him to do this. If they buddied-up, if they became united, they could walk away from this. The thought of that made Michael sick.

"No fucking way," Michael said suddenly. "I couldn't forgive this little fucker for what he's done. I'll pay you forty thousand to kill him right here, right now. I'll even pay you fifty. Do it." Jake was blubbing again, tears practically spurting from his face; his mouth open, wet and dribbling; his huge, baby-eyes gazing up imploringly at Keith; his head shaking. "You little shit," Michael spat. "You think you can kill my wife and daughter and get away with it?"

"I didn't! I didn't kill either of them!"

"You gave my daughter — my *fifteen year old* daughter — drugs. Heroine! You gave it to her, Jake. You supplied it. It killed her. And then my wife killed herself because of what you'd done. You deserve to die. You shouldn't be here on this earth."

"I didn't know she was fifteen!" Jake cried. "She didn't have to take the drugs! Where'd she get the money from? She got it from you! Her dad! Where was he—" he was directing this question at Keith now, trying to get him on-side, "—when his daughter was out taking drugs? He was fucking his secretary, or someone. Eleanor knew that. His wife knew it too! He'd had loads of affairs. His wife didn't kill herself because of me. She was already drinking herself to death because of *him*! They made Eleanor's life hell! That's why she ended up hanging around with people like me. I know I'm scum. But I never wanted to hurt anyone. I never wanted her to die. She wouldn't have been looking for escape if it hadn't been for him!"

Keith allowed a long and icy silence to descend upon the room. Michael felt it smothering him. Keith looked from Jake to Michael, Michael to Jake, and he downed the last of his coffee. At last, he addressed them both with the air of a vicar closing a sermon: "One man in his time plays many parts," he said. The boy looked up at him in confusion, but the meaning settled heavily on Michael. "It's Shakespeare, Jake. You're both as bad as each other, pretending to be righteous, pretending to be hard men, pretending to be this, that and the other," Keith clarified. "Well," he said. "That was all very emotional. But the thing is, I'm here to make some money. Just like you were, Jake, when you sold heroine to a fifteen year old."

"I didn't know ..." his voice tailed off weakly.

"Jake, save it," Keith said, putting his finger on his lips. "I'm going to kill you."

"No, no ..." Jake seemed to have lost his fighting energy. Keith knelt down and pulled from his bag a large, polythene sheet which he flapped out across the floor. Jake, realising what that meant, suddenly went wild, adrenaline propelled into his veins by abject terror. He screamed, high and loud, and Michael watched, the room pulsing with the beat of his heart. He could see every detail of Jake's skin, every sweating pore, every quivering nasal-hair, every lip-crease. Time had slowed. The world had vanished. There was only Jake and Keith, and the tumult inside him. Keith heaved Jake over sideways, onto the polythene sheet, still tied into his chair. He got the knife from the table, showed it to Michael, then to Jake, before kneeling down, stroking the boy's hair with incongruous affection, and then ramming the blade into the boy's chest.

The screaming ceased abruptly. Keith deftly contained the jets of blood in a towel he'd produced from somewhere, and held the blade in place until the boy was still. Panting a little, he stood, leaving the knife where it was, wiping his dripping hands on the towel which he dropped onto the polythene. Then, very slowly and calmly, he reached into the bag and pulled out a Polaroid camera. He took a photo of the body, walked several times round the room shaking the white square which emerged, and then showed it to Michael. "Just a reminder. Proof. So you can't ever doubt your own memories." Michael, viewing the photo through the woolly fug which had formed between himself and the world, nodded. He could tell Keith was talking but could barely hear his words. Keith had to practically shout to get him to respond. Michael felt his eyelids scraping over his corneas as he blinked, heard his own breath roaring in and out across his dry tongue. Then, he vomited into his own lap.

Keith got out an iPad. Using passwords which Michael provided, he logged in to Michael's internet banking account and transferred the agreed fifty thousand.

At last, Keith rolled the body up in the polythene, chair and all. He secured it with duct-tape, and dragged it out of the house without leaving even the tiniest speck of blood on the laminate flooring.

What he did with it then, Michael had no idea. Keith came back for his bag, untied Michael and dropped the sick-covered rope into a plastic sack.

"You were filmed handing the envelope over in the pub," Keith said, "so I would never breathe a word of this to anyone if I were you. You are very much an accessory to murder. It's been a pleasure doing business with you."

Then he was gone. There was the distant sound of an engine, and tyres on gravel. And that was the last Michael saw or heard of Keith.

*

The white transit headed away from the town for a while. Then it pulled off the man road, picking its way through rolling countryside peppered with grubby sheep, and finally, along a dirty track into a dense patch of forest. The Scotsman killed the engine, got out and went round to the side door. He heaved it open and stepped up into the van's dusty interior where the large polythene bundle lay. With difficulty, he unwrapped it, which involved turning the whole heavy lot over several times and pulling the polythene away. At last, the figure lay there exposed, firmly tied to the chair, blinking up at him and grinning.

*

2 weeks earlier

"Barry," the broad, fat man said, shaking hands with his more slender framed friend.

"Greg," Barry said. "It's been a while. Is everything okay? You sounded really worried."

"Yeah. Let's get a drink and I'll tell you about it." The two Cockneys ordered a couple of pints of Pride, Barry paid, and they took a small table in the corner, away from the pool table and the slot machine. "I've got to tell you something," Greg said in his London drawl. "Your boy's in trouble."

"What, again? I thought we'd got it all sorted," Barry said, sighing heavily and running his hand over his mostly bald pate.

"Sorted with the police, yes," said Greg, "but, there's been this posh bloke hanging around in here for a week or so now. Posh blokes stand out like a sore thumb in here. Especially when they're nosing around, asking questions."

"I'm listening," Barry said. He'd known Greg for more years than he could count. They'd been in the Met together; Greg was a Detective Inspector now, and Barry had left to pursue an acting career, much to the amusement of his ex-colleagues.

"Well, it smelt dodgy to me so my ears pricked up."

"I can imagine," Barry nodded.

"So, I made it my business to make his acquaintance, buy him the odd drink, get him talking. He was quite the chatty one after a few bottles of Sol."

"Sol? I didn't even know they sold posh stuff like that."

"Well, it was a surprise to me too. But the point is, he was looking for someone to do a job for him."

"He came to the right place then."

"Naaa, they're all angels in here! Anyway, this wasn't just some small job. He wanted someone taken out."

"Killed?"

"Naaa, wined and dined," Greg said sarcastically. "Yes, of course killed. But he told me why he wanted this bloke killed. You're not gonna like this."

"Ah Jesus, Greg. It was Jake?"

"That's right. The bloke was the dad of that girl; still blames Jake for what happened to the girl and his wife too. He's not gonna let it go neither."

Barry let out a long, pained sigh. His boy had been such a disappointment, but he had no-one to blame except himself. Police work, combined with amateur dramatics, didn't leave much time for parenting.

"I can't really blame the poor bastard," Barry said. "I could kill Jake myself. Seriously. But ... He's my boy. He's a complete fuck-up, but I love him. I can't have some bloke taking out hits on him. How far's this gone? Has he found someone yet?"

"Yeah, Baz, me," Greg grinned. "I said I know someone. I said I could sort it for him. I don't of course. I was just delaying him."

Barry gave a brief laugh. "I could kiss you, Greg."

"Well don't. Let's just work out what we're gonna do now."

"Can we get him put away?"

"It's doable," Greg said. "I could arrest him, and he would go down for it. But a good lad like him? No criminal record, I've checked. He'd have no trouble getting a good defence lawyer. He'd be out in no time. And do you think his little stint inside would help him calm down? In fact, do we really want to put him amongst hundreds of lads with all sorts of dodgy contacts? I think being banged-up would make it easier for him to find someone to do the hit. Someone we don't have any control over."

Barry took several long, controlled breaths, and slurped his pint. Then he took out his phone and called his son. "Jake, I need to see you at home. Now. I'm not joking around."

Twenty minutes later, the three of them were sitting around Keith's kitchen table. Jake was grinning excitedly as if he thought they were about to announce the start of some great adventure. Barry looked at Greg who returned a grave and knowing nod. Then, Barry grabbed Jake's ear and yanked it down to the table, his son gasping now, fingers splayed, helpless.

"You, son, are in trouble," Barry said.

"Alright, Dad! For God's sake! You'll rip my ear off!"

"Then stop grinning and take this seriously. I'm sick of defending you. I'm sick of getting you out of the great big piles of shit you get yourself into. I'm sick of seeing the way you hurt people." He released the ear and Jake sat up slowly, rubbing it. "I don't want to see anyone else hurt. Greg, tell him what you told me."

Greg relayed the story.

"He wants to *kill* me?"

"Well, he wants to get someone else to do the dirty work for him."

"Son," Barry said. "Your life is in danger. And God knows, if you weren't my son I wouldn't get involved. You deserve everything you get. But you are my son and I love you. So ..."

"Dad, I know I've fucked up. I know I've done wrong.

That girl, she died because of me. But you know I'm sorry, don't you? You know I'm going to regret that for the rest of my life."

"Stop grovelling, Jake. This bloke sounds like he'll stop at nothing. He won't rest until you're dead."

"Christ, Dad ..."

"I'm going to send you away. Set you up somewhere. Spain, probably. And you'll have to stay there. I mean, you'll have to stay there for good."

"I don't want to live in Spain," Jake objected. "Not for good anyway."

"That'll take a bit of dough, won't it Baz?" Greg said, ignoring Jake's protestations. "Have you got that kind of dough?"

"No, but I've got an idea that might solve that problem *and* get Jake off the hook." The plan was still forming in his mind, but he was pretty sure it could work. "Like I said, Jake, this bloke isn't going to relax until you're dead. Or until he *thinks* you're dead. Which is where my friend Keith comes in."

"Who the fuck is Keith?" Greg asked, affronted that Barry had a friend he didn't know about.

"Keith ..." Barry paused for dramatic effect, "... is a nasty bastard. Brought up on the mean streets of Glasgow. Huge nose, bushy beard, ponytail."

"How come I've never met him?" Greg said.

"Very few people have," Barry replied.

Jake said eagerly, "How do we contact him?"

Barry gave them both a sly grin. This plan would need some fine-tuning, but his theatre friends would help him lay his hands on the things he'd need. "You want to know who Keith is?" he said, tantalisingly. Then, adopting his best Glaswegian accent, he said, "Boys, you are looking right at him!"

The Viaduct

"Oi! Biscuit!" Joel shouted across the road at the old man, who was walking his dog along the stony path, past the church. He turned for a moment and his face filled with dismay when he saw us. "Biscuit!" Joel called in a mockery of friendliness. We crossed the road and followed him, not quite catching him up, but making sure he knew we were there behind him, sniggering. Biscuit continued away from us, slowly, his left leg dragging as it always did in its built-up shoe. His dog, Snowy, bounced obliviously beside him.

Biscuit was my Grandad. And we were horrible to him. We called him Biscuit because of his limp. Limp Bizkit, one of Joel's favourite bands. It was an ironic nickname, but I don't think Joel had thought beyond the word 'limp'.

It was boring in this town, with its one brief flicker of a high street and nothing else but a few cottages and the village green. That's no excuse, I know. There were other kids that did it too; it wasn't just me and Joel. That's no excuse either. Joel was just one of those people you couldn't say no to. Well I couldn't anyway.

Joel's phone rang. He pulled it from his jeans pocket and answered. I waited for him patiently, and watched Biscuit limp along the path away from us. I was eager for Joel to finish his conversation, but Joel was talking to some girl I didn't know. He was like that, Joel, always on the phone to someone, usually a girl. I don't know how he even managed to get any reception here in the valley, but things just always sort of fell into place for Joel. My phone hardly ever rang. His rang constantly, bringing an endless flow of exciting opportunities into his life. That day, Joel seemed to talk to whoever it was for ages as we walked along behind Biscuit, me beside Joel, Joel in another world with some gregarious character I didn't know. Joel laughed and sniggered and talked about this and that. I didn't really have many mates. Probably because I was the kind of geek who used words like 'gregarious'. I was just pleased that Joel wanted to be my mate, sometimes at least. So I waited for him to finish his conversation. He was always really animated when he was on the phone, laughing with his whole body, waving his free hand about, turning round or stopping unexpectedly and doubling up, which slowed us down so much that a gap opened up between us and Biscuit.

After a while he was back with me, the phone safely stowed in his pocket. But, "See ya later," he said to me, without any further explanation, and headed back the way we'd come.

"Where you going?" I said. "I thought we were going to ..." Biscuit was miles away already, almost out of sight round the bend up ahead.

"I could tell you, but then I'd have to kill you!" Joel grinned, trotting backwards away from me, unable to delay his adventures another moment. And he sped off. I could have followed him, but I knew I wasn't wanted. I wouldn't have any fun with Biscuit all by myself, so I moped my way back up the path, through imagined clouds of Joel's dust.

That night, Biscuit saved my life. He didn't mean to, he

just did, by accident. You see, I was going to end it all.

Yes, you hear me right. I'd had enough. I hated being me. I hated my life. And I'd come to accept that it was never going to change. I was full of a huge, aching darkness, something I couldn't define but which made me feel as if I was poisoned; no, it made me feel as if *I* was the poison, as if I was the one thing that made this bright world bad.

There's a very high bridge across the valley just beyond the edge of town. Used to be a railway bridge. We call it the viaduct, although I'm not sure that's exactly what it is. It's a hell of a long way down to the scrubby bushes on the valley floor though. That would do it. And that's where I went. I climbed over the stone balustrade, and was standing with my trainers on a crumbling protrusion of brick, looking down at the huge, dizzying drop, and I wasn't even scared. That's how I know I would have done it.

But my phone rang. Probably I was in the only spot for miles around where my phone would get any reception. Maybe I was getting exciting phone calls like Joel's all the time but just didn't know it because the only place my phone would get any reception was here, poised on this tiny ledge of brick, on the outside of the viaduct, above a terrifying drop. To be honest though, I did sometimes get phone calls, but usually they were from my mum telling me she was going to be late home and I'd have to cook my own tea. But some part of my mind was always hoping for my phone to ring, as if there was an important call I was waiting for, something that would crop up and change my life. What if this was that call? What if this was something life-changing and exciting? I couldn't just end it all now, without knowing for sure. Even though I was sure I knew it wasn't.

I thought I'd give it one last chance, so I dug it out of my pocket. But in the cold, dry air, I fumbled it, and dropped the bloody thing. I watched it plummet, its little glowing screen flashing like a lighthouse in the twilight as it turned over and over.

I swore. It takes a lot of determination and focus to get to the position I was in; a lot. *I* wanted to die, but *my body* wanted to live, and it had been throwing all kinds of emotions at me to stop me doing what I was going to do, and I'd overcome them all. But this tiny little seed of curiosity was one emotion I just couldn't face-down. I climbed back over the balustrade, angry with myself, and also vividly aware of the irony if I were to slip and fall in the process. Safely back on the bridge path, I peered over and made a note of where the phone must have landed, and slowly made my way down the valley side to retrieve it. It took me a while, and the whole time I was thinking how stupid this was, it was bound to be smashed to bits. Besides, I'd never find it in all those bushes. Even so, I skidded and stumbled my way down to where I thought it must have landed and I started rummaging through the scratchy bushes in the darkness. And it rang again, the screen lighting up like a beacon. I dug it out of the undergrowth which had saved it. Amazingly, it was still in one piece. The screen was cracked and there was mud all over it, but it had had a relatively soft landing.

It was my Mum ringing. *After all that.* I sighed, and looked up at the bridge above me. Then I looked down at my phone, all cracked and muddy.

Mum rang off so I checked my missed calls. All Mum.

I cursed.

And then she rang *again*. I sighed. I answered it.

"Jordan," Mum said, and there was an edge to her voice which told me something was wrong. "It's your grandad. He's in hospital." Her voice was shaky and undulating in ways she couldn't control.

"Oh," I said, not sure how to react. Not sure how I even felt. Right now I was numb, right down inside. I felt like the undead, trapped between worlds. "Is he alright?" It was a stupid question.

"He tried to kill himself, Jord," Mum blurted, crying now. A better mum might have broken that news a little more gently, at a later date perhaps, or not at all. Not my mum. She'd never read that chapter in the parenting manual about how you shield your child from awful realities.

"Okay," I said. "It's okay, Mum. I'm coming home."

*

When I found out what Biscuit had done, I couldn't help feeling there was something darkly predictable about the outcome. He was so out of touch with the modern world, you see. To him, forty miles an hour was, literally, breakneck speed, and brick walls were, well, brick walls. So when he'd sped across the car park in his Ford Fiesta, heading for the wall of the minimart, the last thing he'd expected was that the wall would turn out to be made of some flimsy modern material covered in brick-effect tiles, and that he'd find himself in the toiletries aisle amongst a gathering of bemused shoppers with his face safely buried in an airbag. The most amazing thing is that the surprise didn't kill him.

In the hospital, Mum was distraught, of course. She'd never had a cool head in a crisis. Her makeup was all down her cheeks and her hair all over the place as if she was the one who'd been pulled from the wreckage. You'd have thought he was her own dad, but he wasn't. He was her father-in-law. I tried to calm her down, but she wasn't having any of that. In the end, a nurse came and took her to one side, to give me a break I think.

I peered through the window into the little room where Biscuit was sitting up on a bed, waiting to be given the all-clear. He noticed me, and smiled. He smiled! *After all I'd done to him.* What I did next I did without planning it, or even really wanting to do it: I went in. It was as if my legs knew what needed to be done and had decided to just get on and do it. So in I went.

The door flapped shut behind me, and we just stared at each other.

"Hello Jordan," Biscuit said.

"Hi," I said.

"You okay?"

"I am. Are you?"

And that was when he began to cry.

*

We brought him back to ours and gave him our spare room, until he was feeling better. Mum pandered around him, doing everything she could think of for him, flapping, being overly jolly like some sort of crazed court jester. But it was plain to see she was a flimsy vessel bursting with inner tension, like an aneurism. Stick a pin in her and she'd have popped. I kept out of Biscuit's way for the first few days, and I think he was doing his best to keep out of mine. I walked Snowy for him a few times, just to get myself out of the house really.

I knew I should be feeling horrible with guilt, but I was still numb inside. I couldn't speak to anyone, not Biscuit, not Mum, not Joel. I kept away from everyone, shutting myself away in my room, or staying out by myself, long into the evenings. Mum didn't know it, but I didn't go to school for a week.

Then, one Saturday, Biscuit came into my room. He didn't knock. It was so long since he'd been my age he'd forgotten the sorts of things a boy might be doing alone in his room, but thankfully I was just lying on my bed staring at the posters on the wall, or rather, I was staring through them into imagined blackness.

"Can I come in?" he said, even though he already had. I nodded. "May I?" he asked, and sat down on my computer chair without waiting for an answer. And he smiled at me, the same smile he'd smiled in hospital; the same smile, I now remembered, he'd smiled at me when I was younger, when I used to play games of chase with him among the apple trees in his garden, or when he'd put a steaming bowl of salted porridge on the table in front of me for breakfast when I'd stayed over; the smile he used to smile when he'd finished reading me a story.

I felt as if I was choking.

"We don't see too much of each other these days do we?" he said, deliberately not referring to the times I had seen him out in the street, when I was with Joel.

I shook my head.

"I've missed you very much," he said warmly. I looked at him. I didn't deserve those kind words. "I see you out with the other boys sometimes. Some of those boys are not very nice." I nodded, wanting to look away, but I couldn't. My eyes were doing what my legs had done in the hospital: they knew what was right, and they wouldn't let me look away even though I wanted to. "Boys can be cruel you know," he said.

"Is ..." I began. "Is that why you ...?" I couldn't bring myself to say 'decided to kill yourself', but he knew what I meant. He rolled his head slightly, as if deciding whether to nod it or shake it. "It ... It didn't help," he said at last. "But there's a lot more to it than that too."

I sat up against my pillows. I suddenly realised I was interested. He and I had been about to do exactly the same thing that day. It was weird that we could be so out of touch with each other and yet on exactly the same page. I knew even then that I was to blame for what he'd done, and I know now that I should have been apologising. I should have been desperately trying to make it up to him, trying to find ways of showing him that I cared, that I'd been wrong, that I hated myself for what I'd done. But I just sat there, empty and emotionless. When I sat up to listen to him, it wasn't because of friendliness, fondness, or guilt, it was because I thought that listening to him might help me to understand myself.

"When you reach my age," he said, "you have an awful lot to look back on. Some of it good, some of it ... regrettable. I think ... I think old men are supposed to feel comfortable with themselves. I'm afraid I don't." For a few seconds, he stared through me, at his memories. "I am so alone," he said at last, his pale eyes fixed firmly on me now. That was true; he'd lost his wife, my grandmother, years ago, when I was still young enough to enjoy playing with them both, before I became ...

whatever I had become. "I miss Myra more than it's possible to say," he stated. "And ... Your mother ... I love her as if she were my own daughter, but she has no time for me. She tries, she cares, but she's busy, and I'm in the way. And my only grandson ... Where did he go, eh?" He meant me of course.

Then I said something I really hadn't expected to say. I added someone to his list of people he'd lost. "Your son," I said, flatly and firmly, and I drove it home by adding, "you've lost him too." He took that on the chin, barely reacting, but I heard his breathing change; it was a cruel blow and it had hurt him.

"You're right, Jordan. That's been the hardest of the lot. Your grandmother died loving me; so at least I can find comfort in her memory. Your mother still cares. You ... You're still here, so you might come back to me one day, and I live in hope of that. But your father ... He chooses to have nothing to do with me, or with you, or your mother. But worst of all, it was me who drove him away."

"I know," I stated. "You and him had a massive argument. You were always arguing. So you told him to go away and never come back, and that's what he did." I realised I was sounding petulant and childish.

"I regret it so much now," he said. "I drove my own son away. Your father. You'd have had a father in your life if it wasn't for me. Religion makes people do such terrible things."

I asked the obvious question: "What's *religion* got to do with it?"

Grandad took a breath, as if preparing to dive into a cold river. Or jump off a bridge. "Your father had acted in a way which I found deplorable. I think you're old enough to hear the truth now." I waited, agog. The truth came slowly, falteringly: "He ... He was not a good father. And he was an even worse husband to your mother. And he was certainly no Christian. Not in the way he acted anyway. And me a vicar! I was shamed by him. He drank; he womanised. He made a fool of your mother, and of me, and others too. You'll probably remember the shop he and his friend ran?"

"Joel's dad?"

"Yes. Well, your father embezzled money from it so he could treat his mistress to things your mother could only dream of. Embezzlement is a crime, Jordan. Do you know what it means?"

"Stealing?"

"That's right. Maybe I ... Maybe I shouldn't be telling you this. But ... You need to know what happened, and I need to tell you. The religious community of the village was enraged by him, but I spurred them on in their rage and ... and in the end, we ousted him. My *own son*. I threatened him with prison, and we bullied him away. He couldn't come back here, we'd made his life hell."

I looked at him, and tried to work out what I should be thinking of him. He was someone I had bullied mercilessly, but he was also a bully. Or had been at least. And he was the reason I had that black, heavy sorrow inside me. He was the reason I waited for that imaginary phone call that would change my life.

"So ..." I began, eager for more information now, but not sure what to say to make him continue. But he pulled himself together and continued anyway: "I thought I was in the right at the time, but I've had twelve years to ... to

71

think about my actions." I could see the sadness in him. I could see that heavy weight of sorrow dragging on his innards just like it did on mine. I knew how he felt. He was the man who had pushed me on the swings in the park, made me giggle, walked me to and from school; loved me. He was the man I had come to resent deeply for reasons I could never understand. Children pick up on the tiniest of things, and I must have absorbed some of what had happened.

"I was on the viaduct," I said suddenly.

"What were you doing there?"

I knew I just had to let the story fall out of me in whatever way it liked. Otherwise it would stick in me somewhere, and remain unsaid. "I was going to jump. I was really going to do it, Grandad. I wanted to make it all be over. What Joel and I did to you was so bad. I felt so bad. Not just about that, but about other things too. The emptiness, the constant feeling of emptiness inside me, like I was always hoping for something that would never actually come. And the way I was changing. I wanted it to be over." I realise now, looking back, that I never actually said 'I wanted to kill myself,' just 'I wanted it to be over', a sort of watered down version. Maybe, in the end, I didn't want to kill myself at all. I just wanted a different life.

Grandad's sagging face looked older than ever, as if I was looking at it through a rain-covered window which distorted it, making the loose skin seem to be melting and tumbling downwards, and then he dropped from his stool and knelt beside me, grabbing my hands and sobbing, "Oh my boy, my poor boy ..." I was six again. I let him pull me into him; I let him hold me and we sobbed together.

*

"Is that Snowy?" Joel said as he came bounding up to me a day or two later. I'd taken Snowy out for Grandad, and was just heading along the path past the church. Joel had paused his telephone conversation to ask the question, and even as I replied, he put the phone back to his ear and carried on talking. He walked along beside me and Snowy, sometimes sniggering conspiratorially into the phone, sometimes talking in loud but cryptic phrases. At last, he hung up.

"Biscuit's staying at yours isn't he?" he said, with that edge to his voice that told me he was about to say something derogatory. I felt knotted up inside. I'd known I couldn't go on avoiding him forever, that sooner or later I was going to have to face up to him, to tell him I wasn't going to victimise Grandad anymore. But it wasn't going to be easy. Joel seemed to posses some powerful magnetism that made me want to do things his way, win his approval. If I'm to be completely honest, Grandad didn't posses that. It was a tug-of-war Grandad could not win.

So I had to take control of myself.

"Don't call him that," I said. It came out feebly, and I couldn't even look at Joel as I said it, but at least I did actually say it, and somewhere inside I felt a pang of satisfaction. But Joel's reaction shocked me.

"Okay," he said.

I couldn't believe that was all he was going to say. It left me speechless, and we walked on in silence. But I felt my message had been missed. This was a big thing I was doing, standing up to Joel, telling him not to do the very thing we'd always done. We'd always known it was wrong, and yet we'd chosen to do it, together. We were like partners in crime. You can't just put a stop to something like that with a few feeble words. No, Joel can't have understood what I meant. So I added, "It's just ... He's my Grandad. I'm not going to ... you know ... anymore."

"Okay," Joel said again. "Fine. I only did it because you did it anyway."

"What?" I said. We stopped and faced each other, Snowy bouncing about at our ankles like Tigger.

"Well, he's your grandad," Joel said. "I thought it was weird the way you spoke to him. I'd never speak to my grandad like that, but it's what you always did so I went along with it."

"What?" I said again, feeling as if the whole world had just turned inside out. "But you ... You started it, not me. I was just going along with you. You always took the piss out of his limp."

"Yeah but only because you did."

"You called him Biscuit!"

"So? What's wrong with that?"

"Well, it's not his fault he's got a limp is it?" I said defensively.

"What's 'Biscuit' got to do with that?"

"Limp Bizkit," I reminded him.

"Oh!" he said, and laughed. "Is that what you thought? That's not why I called him it."

"Isn't it? Why then?"

"I dunno. I can't remember." He thought for a moment. "Yes I can. When I was a kid he used to give me a biscuit when I saw him, you know, when he was still the vicar and my dad used to take me to church. I used to cry

I think, so he'd always give me a biscuit, so I always used to say 'biscuit' when I saw him. It sort of stuck from there."

"I thought it was because of his limp."

Joel laughed. "That's brilliant! Limp Bizkit! I'd never thought of that before."

I think he was actually telling the truth. Which meant it was *me* who was responsible for everything we'd done to Grandad. That thought sickened me, and I walked on, briskly, as if I could leave that realisation behind in the cold, damp air. Joel followed.

"What about the others?" I said after a while, meaning the other lads from the village who were horrible to Grandad.

"Yeah they're just idiots," Joel said. "Don't worry about them. I'll talk to 'em."

I thought, 'Yes but how many of them would say they only did it because *I* did it?' That heavy darkness was swelling in my stomach now, the same darkness that had made me want to be someone else, that had driven me to the viaduct that night. I had more to answer for than I'd ever realised.

The silence made the air feel dangerous and I needed to break my thoughts. I told him everything Grandad had said about my dad.

"Well, that's all news to me," Joel said. "Is it true? I'll ask my dad."

"No, don't," I said. "Well, do what you want. It doesn't really matter. It's true. You can't change that now."

"It still doesn't seem like a reason to hate anyone," Joel said. "Wait," and he pulled his vibrating phone from his pocket. He answered it, said a few words, laughed, hung up.

"Did you know he was trying to kill himself?" I said suddenly.

"What? When he tried to turn the Co-op into a drive-through?"

"Yes."

"Because of us?"

"Because of me."

*

It was freezing up on that bridge. I don't know what I was going to do this time. I don't know if I was actually going to jump, or if I was just trying to imagine what would happen if I did. Perhaps I was just reminding myself the bridge was there, like a failsafe. Perhaps I liked knowing that the only thing keeping me in this world was the weathered row of bricks beneath my heels. It was so precarious. And maybe that forced me to consider whether or not being here was better than being dead.

Things were going to be better from now on though. Maybe. Grandad and I understood each other now. I couldn't take back or change all the awful things I'd done, and he couldn't change his past either, but the future would be better. And I had this odd feeling, this strange, prickly sense that there was hope in the air. You see, if Grandad and I could forgive each other, maybe Dad and Grandad could too.

But no, that was inconceivable. This story wouldn't have a happy ending; I didn't deserve one. This was as good as it was going to get. Hope? It wasn't hope at all. It was just wishes that would never come true. That's the way real life goes. I sighed, and in the distance an owl screeched.

I was so deeply lost in these thoughts that, when my phone rang, the shock of it made me lose my footing, my left foot coming off the ledge and waving about in the air. I grabbed the wall behind me and my whole body pulsed like a bolt of lightning.

Finding my footing again, I let out a short, sharp breath. Then, I dug the phone from my pocket, careful this time not to drop it. I saw the words 'unknown caller' on the screen. Weird. I answered it suspiciously.

"Hi," said the voice on the other end of the line. "Is that Jordan?"

"Yes."

"Jordan, um ..." The caller, male, sounded uncertain, nervous even. "I hope you don't mind, you're grandad gave me your number. Look, this is a bit out of the blue, I know, but ... This is your dad."

Sophia Ricotta

The doorbell pissed on my already sputtering creativity, and I thumped the desk. The bottle of cheap whisky staggered and I steadied it, rubbed my burning eyes, and felt myself condense back into cold reality.

Glancing resentfully at my sparse, scribbled notes, and my blank Word document, I ducked through the low doorway and hurried down to the hall. The cold of the flagstones sprouted through my thick socks and I remembered I hadn't switched the heating on. How long had I been up there? It was getting dark already and, automatically, my hand flicked the light switch.

There was a voice from the other side of the door. A once familiar cry.

Oh Christ.

"Siiimon Kendal!" the voice hooliganned through the letterbox to a long-forgotten tune. "Siiimon Kendal! Siiimon Kendal is a horse's arse!" I saw his spindly, yellowed fingers pushing the flap open, his rubbery, wet lips delivering his ridiculous call to arms. I felt as if he had opened a flap in my forehead and was yelling into my skull, rallying my sleeping memories. I heard him grumble something and through the mottled glass panel beside the door I saw his fragmented shape flapping as he beat his arms against his freezing torso. A miserable moment later the flap opened again: "Heee looks like a horse's arse, heeee smells like a horse's arse, heeeee is aaaa horse's ...

Oh for God's sake, Si, hurry up. It's fucking freezing out here!"

I opened the door. Cold swarmed in, and so did Gilbert.

"Yey, y'big tosser!" he foghorned as he gripped me in an icy bear hug and lifted me off the ground. "Shit, man, it's been ... how long?" He ripped off his scarf and gloves and I pushed the door shut. "Hey, man. Good to see ya! Caught you in the middle of anyth—You dirty old bastard. What's her name, eh? Eh! Bit of a saucepot is she? Hey, nice place!" He led himself through to the kitchen leaving me to scoop his coat from the air or let it fall to the floor. "Sorry to just drop in on you unannounced, but ... Wow, nice kitchen!" I took a deep breath, hoisted the heavy camel skin off the floor and hung it on one of the pegs. "No beers in the fridge?" he said, finding out for himself. "I'd've brought some if I'd known. Christ, man, it's colder in here than it is outside! Should've left the fridge open; warm the place up a bit."

"I know," I said, wondering what to do with my ridiculous, fake smile which was beginning to ache.

"Look at you, mate. You look like fucking shit!" He announced that as if he was telling me I'd just won a great prize.

"Thanks." My cheek twitched. He was right though: with my ragged jumper and threadbare cords I must have looked like some sort of ageing art student. At least I wasn't dressed in a cream suit and a pink flowery shirt, like he was.

"Got any skunk, mate?"

He was a good friend, once. We grew up together. I *say* grew up, but I think that's something he never really did.

"No, I er ... don't really ... you know ... anymore."

"What? Come on man, you're a toker." I shook my head apologetically. "Tea then?" He said, pulling out a chair and sitting at the table. "To drink, not to smoke, idiot." My frozen, inane grin hmmfed into a genuine smile.

*

Sophia Ricotta. Sex bomb. Journalist. Sophisticated, beautiful, desired by all men.

That's about all I had. She wasn't going to be called 'Ricotta', of course, but something exotic. I don't know why I was so drawn to this character. She wasn't my usual type of subject. But she'd been swimming around my head all day, taking shape, becoming a personality. All I needed now was a story to put her in. That was the problem. I'd taken a six month sabbatical from teaching to write my second novel but I hadn't come up with a new story for about 2 years, and my agent, who was pretty much the antithesis of Sophia Ricotta, was getting twitchy. That wasn't the only reason I desperately wanted to write, though. Writing took me away from myself. I *became* characters when I wrote; I felt their fears, their pain, their desires ... *Theirs*, not mine. It was true escapism.

But I couldn't seem to do it anymore. It wasn't just writer's block. It was sort of ... life block. I'd always had some vague idea there was something I was searching for, some kind of Nirvana. It had eluded me thus far. I'd tried all sorts of things over the years: travel, relocation, career changes ... Surely the one thing I'd been seeking had to be the one thing I'd been shying away from: settling down. So I'd settled down.

She was wonderful, Lisa. A truly beautiful person: balanced, thoughtful, witty, sexy; you name a positive attribute, she had it.

She left me about two months ago. She took most of her stuff and went to live with a friend. Her beauty and warmth had gone right out of my life, and, insanely, I felt ... relieved.

"...So I thought I'd look you up, mate," Gilbert was saying as he sipped his tea. We were in the sitting room now and I was trying to get the fire to light. He'd been going on for a while about his adventures in Africa, South America and Australia, his last girlfriend, his yachting accident, his ... God knows what else. I had a vague idea I knew some of it already, probably through the local grape vine. The story seemed to have culminated in his running out of money, returning home to England and to good ol' M'maa and P'paa, and his newfound niche as an estate agent.

"Truth is," he said, getting to the bit I'd been subconsciously both suspecting and dreading, "living with Mummy and Daddy's okay for a bit, y'know. I mean, don't get me wrong, 's great actually: meals on the table; no rent, y'know; but it's not ... 'snot cool, man. What if I want to bring a girl back? Can't see old Pops taking very kindly to having scantily clad young ... What am I saying? He'd fucking love it! Mum'd have his eyes out though, and his bollocks for earrings ... So ..." He left it at that, and it was only after a long silence that I realised he felt he'd actually asked me something. I prodded the fire a bit more, playing for time. "Y'know, mate," he went on, flicking a curtain of hair back dramatically, "it'd be like old times! Like the summer of '95! You look like you could do with having a rocket shoved up your social life. You supply the weed, I'll bring the girls!" He clapped his hands and lurched backwards in his chair as if it had just accelerated suddenly. He laughed in a hearty, knowing kind of way which waned awkwardly in the absence of my response. "Come on, mate, I hear you've got a spare room. It'd be a laugh, like old times." Christ, the last thing I needed was this maniac taking over my life. I had to get my head round my writing.

"Oh!" I said as if I'd just got what he was on about. He gazed at me, his brown eyes glittering excitedly. "It would be great, but ..."

"Man, you're a mate. Think of it, the Dynamic Duo back in action!"

"But I don't have a spare room."

"You don't have ... But my mum said your mum told her ..." He was still grinning expectantly. He wasn't going to let go of hope that easily.

"Sorry mate," I said, "but I just took on a lodger."

"Really? Your mum know about this?" Even now, his look of excited anticipation didn't leave him.

"Gilbert, not all of us have to report our every move back to Mummykins, you know."

"Fuck off!" he laughed. "Well, who you got then? This happen recently? Anyone I know?"

"You only know crack heads and sex addicts, and none of them made it past my rigorous interview process. No, just got it sorted out this morning, actually." The lie was coming easily to me now. If only I found it this easy to invent a story when it came to my writing.

"Oh yes?" he said, adopting a sideways, conspiratorial expression. "A woman?" And he made one eyebrow bounce up and down slyly.

"No, no. Ah ..." I thought about it for a moment. He was going to want details, so I needed to come up with some pretty quick. Suddenly it came to me: someone exciting, even by Gilbert's standards; someone he definitely didn't know. "... Ah, well, yes actually. A friend from work. A girl. Her name's Sophia Ricotta."

*

Once upon a time we were inseparable. He was a laugh. Back then, being stupid was an essential part of life. He hadn't changed, hadn't moved on, hadn't settled down, or even *tried* to settle down. I envied him that though. Life was still an open book to him. A ridiculous farce of a novel, in fact. He hadn't yet reached the chapter where life becomes meaningless, or at least, where meaninglessness becomes a problem rather than a bad-behaviour-licence. He still had the security of untapped possibility ahead of him. Even if he did develop that "what's it all about?" feeling, he could relax, safe in the knowledge that he hadn't tried everything yet.

Gilbert turning up had suddenly reminded me how complete I wasn't.

"Christ, mate," he said when I'd finished extolling Sophia's virtues. "She sounds like a babe!" She did too. I'd described her vividly: her strong, curvaceous figure; her intelligent, subversive sense of humour; her healthy appetite for uncomplicated sex. "When the hell can I meet her?"

Oh shit.

"Well," I said, hoping to God my writer's block would not extend to everyday lies, "um, she ... is hardly ever here.

Or," I suddenly remembered she was only supposed to have moved in this morning, "I mean she will be. She does a lot of charity work in her spare time." I was kicking myself before he even began to respond.

"Oh, ho, man. Charity work? This bird sounds unreal. A proper babe. If I don't get her into bed any time soon, I'll die!"

*

And that's how I inadvertently secured Gilbert as a permanent fixture in my life.

Sophia, of course, was never there, but that didn't deter him. I thought he'd get bored, but he didn't. He was forever asking about her, peeking about, looking for signs of her. I started to worry he'd realise the truth, so I began dropping items around the place which I claimed were hers: a Coldplay CD on the arm of the sofa; a pair of fishnet tights hanging over the edge of the laundry box in the bathroom; a stick of dark lipstick; a hairbrush; all Lisa's of course, but Gilbert didn't know that. He just lusted after Sophia, and hungrily swallowed every word I fed him about her. She was shaping up quite well in my mind too. I'd imagine her perfect arse flicking left and right beneath the silk kimono she would surely wear about the house of an evening; her long, shiny hair smelling of silk and apples as she brushed past me in the hall. And she wasn't just sexy in a physical way. She had a self-assuredness, a certainty about her place in the world, and a lust for life which nothing could dampen.

Now that I had Sophia, I would surely be able to get moving on my novel. I had Gilbert to thank for that, at least. So I lost myself in her world, imagining how she spent her time, who her friends were, who she fucked, *how* she fucked, but no actual story came. My mind cramped, an exhausted muscle. The only thing that could massage it was whisky. How I needed that burn. How I needed to feel hollowed out like a lightning tree for a moment, but it was *only ever* for a moment.

*

Chunks of ugly noise juddered through Sophia Ricotta's world. Had I been asleep? I'd certainly had my face on my desk; I'd certainly dribbled.

I grabbed the phone and struggled to see who was calling. My eyes were hot coals.

"Hello," I managed, and suddenly noticed the acrid smell of my own arm pits.

"Simon," came my agent's affectionless voice, her flabby second chin so thick around her throat it gave her the timbre of someone struggling to swallow a gluey lump of Brie.

"Oh, Joyce, great to hear from you," I managed, finding it surprisingly hard not to slur.

"I'll get straight to the point," she said. I felt my skin ice over. "I'm going to need to see something from you very soon. I'll be honest with you. Sales from your first book are not so high that you can afford to take liberties with me." Suddenly I was sober. "I'll need a couple of chapters by the end of the month. Sooner, if you have them. Do you have them?"

"Do I have them? Well, um ... yes, of course! First couple of chapters. Yes, sure. I'll ... I just need to ..."

"Write them?" she said flatly.

"Yes. Mmm."

"Then please do so and send me them. Happy writing."

*

Two days later, Lisa called round to collect the last of her things. She'd changed her hair, had it cut short so it cupped her face. She'd lost weight too, mostly off her hips and breasts, which was a shame because she used to be quite curvaceous.

"I see you've not managed to kick the whisky then," she said, coldly. "Or rather, I *smell* you haven't."

I'd just had time to put the few items I'd borrowed back in the box upstairs where she'd left them, and now I felt a strange sense of anger: why was she taking Sophia's CD? Sophia's tights? Sophia's brush?

When I finally shut the door behind her, I realised I couldn't remember the last time I'd washed.

*

I restocked Sophia's things the next day. I couldn't have Gilbert asking awkward questions, and besides, it might help me understand her better. For my story. When I got back, I emptied the shopping bags out onto the bed in the spare room and put everything away where I thought Sophia would want them. Going through them, I was shocked at how much I'd bought: shoes and skirts and stockings and makeup and knickers and eyelash curlers and perfume and ... Some of it I couldn't even remember buying, but I was lost in her now. I'd have a story soon, I was sure of it. I decided to fuel my creativity with a small whisky. And after my third or fourth large one, I fell asleep at my desk.

I awoke in Sophia's room, my head thumping. It was two o'clock in the morning, and when I went down stairs to neck a gallon of water, I realised that, at some point in my drunken stupor, I'd tidied the kitchen.

*

I didn't see much of Gilbert for two or three weeks. I think he was giving up on Sophia. But that didn't stop me feeling the need to buy more and more things for her, and leave them scattered around the place. Somehow, she seemed to balance up the inexplicable wrongness I felt in my life.

The doorbell yanked me from my warm stupor. I wasn't at my desk where I should have been. I was in Sophia's room. For a moment the whole place rotated and everything waltzed round me in couples. I forced my eyes to widen and the waltzing stopped. The doorbell was hammering out a relentless rhythm and I heaved my dishevelled self off the bed.

Sophia's room.

It was perfect now: decked in neutral colours, but accented in pinks and oranges; a variety of patterned cushions, all different, yet matching; a wicker chair with a couple of old teddies reclining on it; a chest of drawers speckled with little pots of makeup and tea lights; on the wall a pop art poster, the one with the full red lips all done in dots like a close up of a comic strip; opposite it a huge photo of New York in black and white but with yellow taxis; on the vanity unit before the large mirror which was edged in twinkly fairy lights, a pair of furry handcuffs and a huge knobbly vibrator. I touched these last two, about to hide them away in a drawer, but decided against it.

I don't quite know why I always bothered to answer the door to Gilbert, except that I was beginning to enjoy the Sophia-fantasy. I loved hearing him lust after this girl he'd never seen; I loved building her character up a little more each time, adding a new lie, adding new depth.

"Christ mate, you look wrecked," were his first words to me. "Been burning the candle at both ends? How's it coming on then, the novel?"

"Yeah, okay, thanks," I lied.

Soon we were sitting in the front room sipping coffee as Gilbert went on about how wonderful his life was, who he'd had sex with lately, and his recent promotion. I managed to stop myself asking why he was still living at home with his parents.

He asked if Sophia was in, of course. Today, it turned out, she was at T'ai Chi. That was news to me, but it fell out of my mouth before I had time to think. Apparently, she was also stopping over at a friend's tonight. Her friend was a fashion designer and wanted to get Sophia on the catwalk in her next show. I could see Gilbert redden with desire.

He tossed something down on the coffee table. Two small cards. They slid to halt on the face of some young woman who was busy adorning the cover of Cosmo. Succumbing to his will as usual, I flipped them over and saw they were his business card. He grinned and nodded.

"Just got them," he said. "Whaddya think?"

"Why two?"

"One for Sophia. Tell her to call me!"

*

The following week, I had a phone call from my agent

telling me she was no longer prepared to wait. Either I put something in the post to her that day or I was dropped. I told her I'd posted something just yesterday, special delivery, and I couldn't believe it hadn't arrived. Afterwards, I literally ran upstairs to write it.

Several hours later I was descending into an alcoholic abyss, the blank Word document before me making me snowblind. Stung back to life by my mobile's frenzied chiming, I grabbed it and answered, rude and cross.

Oblivious now to my curtness, Gilbert announced, "I've got a date with your Sophia tomorrow."

"Sophia?"

"*Oh* yes. We've been in contact a fair bit over the last couple of days. Don't sound so surprised. She told me she got my details from you."

"Sophia ... *Ricotta*?"

"Yeah! The babe who likes a bit of three-way! She writes a filthy email, I can tell you. Quite a way with words!"

"I never said she likes three-way."

"Said she'd heard all about me, seen photos of me, wants to meet up! God knows what you said to her, mate, but I'm taking her out tomorrow, *at last!* Can you believe it? After all this time, *she* wants *me*!"

I opened and closed my mouth a few times but couldn't find any words. Maybe Gilbert had guessed I'd invented Sophia to get rid of him and was mocking me now.

I found myself suddenly excited, as if I believed she had somehow actually come into being, like a metaphysical version of 'Weird Science'. Typical then, if that was the case, that she should go for Gilbert, not me.

Numbed, confused, I wished him luck, and arranged to speak to him after the date.

*

Sophia flicked her dark hair, perched on a bar stool and ordered a glass of red wine.

That must be him propped against the fruit machine at the far end of the bar, as they'd arranged. He was drinking some sort of colourful cocktail and trying to look as if he hadn't been stood up. His face was deep pink. He'd loosened his tie and slopped some of his cocktail down the front of his suit. Sophia eyed him over the rim of her wine glass and decided she'd left him suffering long enough.

She slipped through the crowd, keeping out of his field of vision and approached him from behind. She slid her hand over the curve of his bum, and blew on his ear.

He straightened, pulling his shoulders back and his stomach in, making himself erect. He leaned into her as she licked his ear, emitting a playful laugh.

He rolled his head and groaned. "Sophia?"

"Hello," she whispered, running a fingertip down his cheek and over his lips. He licked it, sucking it in and rolling his tongue around it.

"At last." Slowly, he turned. It seemed to take him several seconds to focus as he looked her up and down.

But he seemed less enthusiastic than she had expected. Confused. Taken aback, even.

Then his expression darkened. He stepped back, looking at her coldly now, and with visible anger.

"I don't fuckin' believe ..." he began, then laughed. "It's a joke, right?"

Sophia felt the burn of humiliation.

Gilbert spat on the floor. "Fuck!" he barked, and wiped his mouth. *"You fucking arsehole. Why ...?"* He was visibly struggling to calm himself as people began to stare. *"Think I'm some sort of shirt-lifter? I thought you were a mate!"*

"You're drunk. Sssh."

"Don't fuckin' 'shush' me, you fuckin' ..." But his fury went beyond words. Suddenly he punched her full in the mouth. She staggered backwards, but she didn't fall. She straightened, and dabbed her split lip with the back of her hand.

Gilbert was panting, red faced and savage. They had an audience now, and one of the barmen was shouting. Sophia had hesitated long enough. She returned the punch, spinning Gilbert round and sending him sprawling across a table. The people around her gaped. She turned, pivoting elegantly on her toe, and the awestruck crowd parted before her as she strutted towards the door.

*

I woke, naked, in Sophia's bed. How the hell had I got there? The last thing I remembered was that bizarre phone call from Gilbert followed by the opening of a new bottle of Bell's. The room wheeled slowly, and my head was tender and empty.

I sat up on the edge of the mattress and rubbed my face.

Something hurt. I probed around my mouth with my fingers, exploring my swollen lip, and wondered how on earth that had happened.

I stood there for a timeless while, trying to remember.

Later, I took a shower, and when I'd finished dusting myself down with talc, I got dressed, *squeezed herself into her favourite skirt, and put her face on. Perhaps she'd go into town this morning. It was a beautiful day, and there was that strappy pair of Jimmy Choos in Selfridges that she'd had her eye on for ages.*

The Atheist

When I lost my faith I thought I couldn't go on. But I did go on. I stood up there every Sunday morning, and told people what they needed to hear. I offered guidance and love, though I felt empty. I couldn't tell them there was no God.

In the past, I did God's work. But if there was no God, what was I supposed to do? I had no purpose.

It was my mother who set me back on my feet again. One day, I confessed to her my loss of faith. It was the hardest thing I'd ever had to do; my mother was a God-fearing Christian. How could I tell her that the thing she'd always seen as the greatest gift a mother can give, the belief which had formed the backbone of my life, no longer meant anything to me? But, slowly, I did, and her answer surprised me.

"Then you are free of it. I'm pleased for you."

I was confused. Was she tricking me somehow? Would this turn into some sort of deeply cutting admonishment?

"Free of it?" I said.

"Of course. Now you can discover your true motivation."

"What do you mean by that?" I asked, feeling like the child she'd read the bible to and imbued with the security of religious dedication all those years ago. She made the moment last by carefully filling my teacup and offering me a slice of simnel cake, which I turned down, eager to receive her wisdom instead. At last, she began. "Your father was an atheist." This was a blow. My father died before I was born, and although my mother had told me much about him, she'd never told me that. Was she about to blame him for my blasphemy, as if I'd inherited it from him, like my bad temper and my competitive streak? "And he was the most Christian man I've ever known," she said warmly. This certainly was not looking like the admonishment I'd been bracing myself for. "Listen, my innocent, infant man," she went on with the hint of a smile. "You do so many good things. That soup kitchen you run; why do you do that? For God?"

"Well," I said after a moment of thought and a sip of tea. "Perhaps. That's what I would have said a year ago anyway."

"Then you're free to do something else, now that you know there's no God."

"Mother," I said, placing my cup carefully down on the slightly cracked saucer. "Are you saying ... Are you saying you don't believe either?" I felt a surge of irritation. Surely she'd not knowingly filled my childish head with stories and beliefs she knew were nonsense? Surely she hadn't raised me on lies?

"I don't believe in a person called God," she smiled, "a conscious being who watches us all and decides our fates. No I don't."

"Well, no, I don't either. I mean, I didn't, even ... before."

"You did once."

"Only when I was a child. I've dedicated my adult life to studying the nature of God. I moved on from that ... over-simplified personification of God a long time ago."

"And now you've moved on again," she stated, and her expression suggested she was waiting for me to see the obvious truth she was presenting me with. But I couldn't! And her patience made me cross now. "Mum, just tell me what you mean," I said, and, embarrassed at the anger in my voice, I felt myself colouring.

"Look, what about that novel you've always wanted to write? Or that round-the-world trip you used to talk about? Or you always wanted to be a vet, didn't you? Now you can do any of those things. There is no God, so you don't have to serve Him anymore. You can do your own thing. You can leave the church."

I was about to take a sip of tea but I found myself lowering my cup and letting some of those ideas swirl before me. But my mother hadn't finished.

"In fact, now that you know there's no God, you don't need to feel constrained by ... by the need to be *good* anymore!"

"I don't do good things just because I feel I *have to*," I said, my frustration driving me to speak before thinking, and I suddenly realised this was the crucial point she had been working towards.

"Not now that you don't believe in God anyway. You're free." She didn't mean I was free to write a novel, or go round the world or become a vet. She meant I was free to act without fear of offending a God I'd always felt was watching me; I could do what I liked now, without the fear of divine judgement and the threat of damnation. "You can even give up the soup kitchen if you like." She was right. I could. I wouldn't be judged. I wouldn't be damned. There was no God for me to justify myself to. I began to entertain the idea of exploring exciting new avenues; I felt thrilled by this opportunity. I felt released, but only for a fleeting moment. "I can't stop the soup kitchen," I said.

"Why not?"

"Because ... Because of the people it helps."

"Because of love," she clarified, and squeezed my hand. Slowly I realised. Even though I had been set free from the shackles of my belief, I wouldn't change my life; I wouldn't stop doing the things I felt were important; I'd just do them for different reasons now, and that tiny thing that no-one else would ever even be aware of was, to me, such a crucial and poignant adjustment that it thrilled me. If I help a man now, I do it for him, not God, not for the salvation of my eternal soul. I do it for the love of my fellow man.

My mother was still gazing at me, as if I hadn't quite understood her message yet. The lines around her eyes deepened as a warm smile grew, and then she glanced upwards, directing my gaze. Still confused, I looked up at the small, colourful letters I had stitched into a piece of Binca when I was a child, and which had hung, framed and yellowing, on the wall above the kitchen hatchway for the last thirty or so years. "God is love," I breathed, and mother's message almost knocked the wind from my lungs. It was a long while before I realised I was grinning. For months, I had been labouring under the immense burden of atheism. But now? I couldn't have understood my mother's revelation – I would never have felt it in a meaningful way – if I'd not been so certain that there was no God. God does not exist, of that I am still convinced. But Love does. And God is love. Atheism freed me, and enabled me to believe again.

Hold-up

I used to spend a lot of time in that particular second-hand bookshop. I liked to lose myself in its dark recesses among the dusty tomes which teamed with tales of drama and courage. I'd put my headphones on and disappear. With my world filled by blaring guitars and roaring death metal vocals so I couldn't even hear my own footsteps or breathing, I felt as if I was not quite part of the reality around me. It was like playing a video game of my own life. Just the way I liked it.

But I remember the last day I ever went in there as clearly as if it was happening right now. That day was life-defining.

I'd been kneeling down for some forgotten period of time, exploring the covers of two books, eagerly soaking up the clues they offered me about their content whilst a dark musical maelstrom thundered in my ears. I would never open a book before I'd bought it. That would just feel wrong. This wasn't a library. I didn't come here to read; I came here to choose, and to buy. A little drop of my meagre wage earned from heroically rescuing abandoned trolleys from the Tesc0 car park, would find its way into the coffers of this place. It was like I was feeding it. And I loved the choosing almost as much as I loved reading the books.

But, my god, something changed that day.

Some sixth sense caused me to glance over my shoulder. Just a quick twitch of the head; I hardly knew I was doing it. And I was gazing back down at the books before I even began to process what I'd seen. A couple of figures standing at the counter which was a fair distance away. But there was something wrong. The image crystallised in my mind and I turned my head really slowly this time, my heart pounding so powerfully I could almost hear it over my music.

A shotgun pointing right at the girl behind the counter. Animated gesticulations from the two hooded figures. Slow mo. The thick quagmire of music muddied the world — I was detached.

One of the men grabbed the girl and dragged her by the arm out from behind the counter, the other man keeping the shotgun trained on her the whole time. I didn't know this girl, she was new. I'd nodded her a greeting when I came in but I'd noticed very little about her, except that she was older than me, plain, verging on ugly, and she was pregnant.

It was clear the two men had not seen me. I was in a dark corner, dressed in my long black coat, black hair, black jeans. I was a patch of shadow, and this place was full of those.

But I need to tell you why I had this fascination for books. I need you to know, so you can fully understand what I was going through. I am a coward. I don't mean 'a bit timid'. I don't mean 'scared of men with shotguns' just like everyone else; I mean my life is governed by fear. Okay, I can go out of the house, do my shopping, live a normal life without anyone guessing, but I'm what you might call a functioning totalphobic. I'm afraid of little things like what people think of me, right through to big things like plane crashes. But what terrifies me most is coming face to face with someone who wants to do me harm. I fear pain, and I fear people who don't. I know that if I met someone who really wanted to hurt me, I'd be too weak with fear to be able to stop them. My mind would flood with images of what might be about to happen, and I'd live the horrors before they'd even begun, imagining my skin tearing, bones breaking, organs rupturing, nerves severing ... And it wasn't just that. It was the thought of my mind and my soul ceasing to exist, as if I'd never had a thought, never dreamed, never loved or laughed or larked about. A universe exists inside every one of us. When you die, what happens to it?

That's why I love reading real life stories, biographies and autobiographies of people who have faced up to horrendous dangers, endured unendurable suffering, kept their heads, and survived. The books I read are about real heroes, real men and women who have put themselves in danger of torture, injury, death, to save others. How can anyone do that? I'd be a pathetic, gibbering mess, my head filled with powerfully imagined experiences of horror as I cowered, waiting for my fate. I have no strength in my arms and shoulders. If you wanted to, you could cut my throat, or twist my arms until the shoulders dislocated. You could break my neck while I tried to elbow you off with increasingly feeble blows. You could slice me open and pull out my innards, I wouldn't be able to stop you. And these are the things that have happened to so many real people in the past, and probably are happening to people in the present, right now, right this second, so why shouldn't they happen to me?

So, when I realised what was happening behind me, I went ice cold, and vomit rose in my throat driven by my pathetic terror. All I could think was 'Please don't see me.' The world spun to the sounds of satanic vocals and insanely fast drums. Nothing felt real.

They dragged the girl and shouted at her. I had no idea what they were saying. I had no idea what they wanted. I was just glad it was *her* they had and not *me*. I was paralysed. I was looking in on another world. My mind was a block of ice, all my thoughts frozen solid. The only thing that kept going was the music, pounding and roaring and reminding me I wasn't dead.

A brave person would have realised they had the advantage here. A brave person would have sneaked up behind the man with the gun and smashed something over his head. Or even, tried to slip away to get help. But all I could think of was the damage a shotgun can do to a person. I imagined that dense cloud of tiny lead balls smashing into my gut, ripping me open, forcing my bowel out of my back in bits. Or what if he aimed higher? My jaw could be sheered off, my eyes peppered with shot, bursting them. Or lower? My penis, my testicles ... I saw it all happening to me even as I crouched, books still in hand. All this had probably taken just a few seconds.

And suddenly something changed. The sharp, bright sting of reality was all over me as if I'd become fully awake. I could hear the men now, they were yelling, "Where's the safe? Where's the fucking safe?" One of the men went round the back of the counter and disappeared through a door leaving the gunman alone with his terrified hostage. My whole being tingled, my ears rang, and it was several long, slow seconds before I realised my music had stopped. I think my phone battery had run out, but I didn't process that at the time. I just found myself removing my headphones and, for some reason, standing up.

And that's when he saw me.

"Who the fuck are you?" he said. Even from here, even through the stocking which smoothed his face into a blur of orange tan, I could see he was as nasty as cancer. He didn't care who he hurt; he'd come here to rob the place and I was in his way. If this was a film, it would be a film about him, and I'd be just some background character getting blown away before you'd even noticed me. I knew I was about to die in a red fog of my own exploding flesh.

But he still had the gun on the girl, as if he could tell I was no threat. And I suddenly imagined, in vivid Technicolor, what would happen to mother and foetus if that gun went off now.

Christ, I did not have the mettle to survive this. I was not Oscar Schindler. I was not Grace Darling or Mary Seacole or the people who hid Anne Frank, or the man who broke into Auschwitz. I would be one of the unremarkable, unremembered, unheroic dead. I was crippled by over-thinking.

I was numb all over. Just like when I was hiding myself inside my music, I could no longer feel my heart beat or hear my own breathing. Fear was shutting me down. Fear was killing me. I was floating.

I'd gone beyond terror, into a world where all I could do was see and hear. I could no longer feel a thing. Not even ... Not even fear. It was like emerging into a brightly lit cavern at the back of a dark cave. I blinked. I breathed. I spoke.

"She's pregnant," I said. It seemed like someone else's voice.

"What?" the gunman said.

I knew that one of those horrible things was going to happen to me now, but I was numb all over, inside and out, and I wasn't thinking about them, I was just thinking about getting that gun away from the pregnant woman.

"Look," I said. "I'm not going to try anything." I raised my hands to show him I was only holding books. "You've got the gun, I'm trying not to shit myself, so I'm not going to try anything, but please don't point the gun at her, she's pregnant."

He spun the gun towards me and yelled, "Get down on the floor. Get on the fucking floor!" That was the end of my moment of bravery. Terror came flooding upon me once again. As I hurriedly knelt, dropping the books and clasping my hands over my head, I heard the roar of the shotgun, I felt the crowd of hot leaden beads surging into my flesh, ripping my face and neck apart and severing my spine ...

But that was just my imaginings. What really happened was this: the woman smashed a champagne bottle candle stick over the gunman's skull and he collapsed. Anticipating the gun firing as he fell, I lurched to one side with a resounding whimper, but the gun did not fire. Then, the girl went back round the counter and slammed and locked the door to the back rooms where the other man had gone. I was on the floor not far from where the gunman lay. I knew I had to get the gun away from him, but my mind reeled with tales of what would happen if he awoke before I got to it, or even, if he awoke when I'd already got it. What would I do? I wouldn't shoot him!

But he might shoot me. It seems such an easy, obvious decision when you read this sort of thing in a book, but fear had me paralysed again, like a huge, invisible being pinning me down.

I couldn't move.

But I knew I had to move.

And, against my expectations, I found I could.

I dived for the gun. The gunman's eyes flickered open and he groaned. I dragged it away from him by the barrel. Terrified it would go off in my hands, I turned it towards him, shaking. I felt as if I was crawling with spiders. I couldn't pretend I was some hard man. I wouldn't be able to frighten this man, so I levelled with him. I said, "I won't kill you but if you move I'll shoot your feet." Where that came from I don't know. He could see I was shaking but that probably made him realise there was all the more chance of the gun going off whether I meant it to or not. I had it pointed at his scruffy trainers, and I slid my index finger over the two triggers. I didn't know if I really would do it, and I hoped I wouldn't find out.

I felt ridiculous, standing there with a shotgun trained on a criminal like some sort of hero. My hands were shaking uncontrollably now, and cold reality made me want to vomit. This wasn't over yet. I knew I was going into shock, and I knew the guy could decide to get up any moment. Would I shoot his feet if he did? I really didn't know. But those real life heroes I'd read about must all have found themselves in a situation like this, not knowing how it was going to end, not knowing if they were going to live or die, if the biography would be about them or about the man or woman beside them. In the end, bravery doesn't save you. Fate does. And fate is utterly random. I wouldn't survive this just because I was the goodie and the man on the floor was the baddie. It was still anybody's game.

But fate was on my side today. The guy's eyes closed and his bleeding head dipped reluctantly onto the floorboards. The blow had been a mighty one, and he had only surfaced from unconsciousness for a few moments. Now, he was falling, inexorably, back into oblivion.

The police arrived. I hadn't even noticed the girl phoning them. There were no sirens, none that I'd noticed anyway, just a sudden influx of uniformed officers.

The girl. She was the hero. She had knocked the gunman unconscious and locked the other man in the back rooms. A pregnant girl. I felt a warm flood of admiration for her. Beyond the wall of policemen around me, I noticed she was lifting her skirt unceremoniously and wiping her legs with some tissue a WPC kept handing her. Her waters must have broken, I realised, and my head filled with ridiculous fantasies about how she'd name her child after me, and I'd be its godfather, and ...

"What?" the girl snapped belligerently when she saw me watching. "Weed myself, didn't I. Oh, and I'm not pregnant neither, cheeky bastard. Just fat."

Not pregnant? I almost laughed. But what would I have done if I'd realised that at the time? It was the thought of her unborn child which had driven me to speak to the gunman, which had given her chance to knock him out. If it wasn't for that misunderstanding, that might not have happened. Things might have been very different.

A policeman relieved me of the shotgun and someone wrapped one of those silver blankets round me. I was clearly in shock by now. The gunman was stretchered away by an ambulance crew. The other man in the back rooms had found his way out and was gone, but apparently he hadn't got the valuable first edition he'd come here for.

I never went in the bookshop again after that. Not because I was afraid of the same thing happening again. And not because I was embarrassed to see the fat woman I'd thought was pregnant. I never went in there again because my fascination for real life acts of bravery had suddenly gone. It wasn't that I had become brave, far from it. But I had been in a life and death situation. I'd faced something I'd always thought I'd be hiding from forever, and I'd acted. I will always be afraid of physical harm, but I know now that I'd always been more afraid of something else. Without knowing it, I'd been afraid of myself. I wasn't any more.

I still keep myself plugged into the raging, deafening blackness of death metal though. It makes the world go away.

Tattoo

Without really meaning to, he gave her an angry scowl. It wasn't that he hadn't appreciated the way she'd dabbed the custard from his chin for him with the corner of his serviette, and it wasn't that he didn't like the gentle way she tried to ease the anguish of his dying dignity with her kind words; it wasn't that she patronised or spoke down to him like some of the other nurses, and she certainly didn't ever ignore his needs, or tend to him with anything other than kindness and selfless cheer, even when he'd messed the bed and needed cleaning up, or when his false teeth fell out unexpectedly, all covered in semi-chewed sprouts and peas, and landed in her lap. No, his scowl had come from deep within.

She didn't know he had once been a young man, vibrant and excited about life, strong and brave, gallant and dashing. She didn't know he had crawled on his belly through the filth of French farmland, silently stalking German officers, and knifing them open in the dark; she didn't know he had single-handedly taken out a Nazi gunnery team who manned an anti-aircraft gun on the outskirts of Paris, before destroying the gun itself, and laying several mines which later tore apart a staff-car killing a prominent Nazi commandant and his henchmen.

She knew none of this. To her, he was just a helpless old man, a wreck, a wraith. But that wasn't what had drawn the scowl from his sagging lips and heavy brow.

It was the fact that he'd tried to look down her top, to lose himself in the soft, warm cleft between her plump breasts, only to see the tip of a tattoo he'd never noticed before. This upset him. He'd thought he knew her. He'd thought that when she smiled at him, she was giving him a piece of her, opening herself to him in friendship and love, saying, "I know things have gone a bit crap for you recently, but I'm here to take your pain away. While you are trapped within this body, I'm trapped within these walls, because unless I'm here helping you, making you feel comfortable and cared for, I am nothing." But she had a tattoo. A big one too, by the looks of it. Right on her breast. He didn't know her at all, and she wasn't a prisoner within these walls. She was young and vibrant and exciting. And this was just a job.

Dream Wedding

It had all been a dream, thank God. No, a nightmare. That sickening moment of revelation; the horror on Julie's face; the vicar standing there open-mouthed; two hundred eyes burning into me with anger, disappointment, hatred ... The image faded. My head was killing me, but a headache I could live with. I couldn't live without Julie.

And I wouldn't have to. As the horror of our wedding vanished, and I allowed myself to drift through the dark, peaceful realm between dreams and reality, I knew my secret was safe.

But suddenly, my reverie was torn apart and the bright lights of the crowded church savaged their way back into my eyes. With a sharp in-breath, I was wrenched awake again, but this time I smelled blood. I struggled to raise my exploding head from the cold steps where I lay. Dizzy and confused, I looked up at Julie. The anger in her eyes hurt me more than the wound on my head. She just dropped the brass candlestick, and walked away from me, back up the aisle.

The relief, the inner peace? *That* had all been a dream.

And I Wish
I'd Asked Why

Just a few years ago, I was a different person: your typical, directionless and carefree student. Until one event made me re-evaluate *everything*.

I had always been one of those rare characters who have no hang-ups, who is what you might call 'well-rounded' and 'balanced'. I don't mean that conceitedly; I'm not saying I was particularly nice, but I was self-assured, uninhibited and unencumbered by inner frustrations, and happy. I'm talking in the past tense, of course.

I was the complete polar opposite of Marcus. A more encumbered, inhibited, frustrated character I have never met, which is probably what attracted me to him. I'd known I was gay since I was about thirteen and I'd never had a problem with it. Even though I wasn't particularly camp or anything, somehow my family seem to have known since I was much younger than that, and they accepted it fully and unquestioningly, so it was never something I had to battle with or suppress. Unlike Marcus. It was only when he'd been at uni for a while that he actually came out, although his sexuality was blatantly obvious to all who met him. He'd spent years acting gay and pretending he wasn't, pretending he was just an eccentric, troubled soul. It turned out he was all of those things.

We were both studying art. Predictably, my art was controlled and detailed and totally lacking in mood or expression, and his was wild and unkempt and vividly expressive, much like his hair. I found him fascinating. And, one drunken night, he found his way into my bed, although nothing happened and we both awoke the following day fully clothed and a little bashful. Then, in the cold light of the morning after, I casually seduced him.

The first time I met him though, he was sitting cross-legged on the concrete floor of the art studio which would soon come to feel like home to all of us. His bony knees protruded through ragged holes in his tight black jeans, and he had the hood of his green, canvass jacket up around his face. He was making charcoal marks on a large piece of paper: great, sweeping, messy marks which he smudged with the palm of his hand and built up in layers of black and grey, dust swirling in eddies across the paper. Every so often he would rub away at a bit of it with a gummy rubber, or he'd add to it with the charcoal, darkening an area carefully. That amused me because he worked on those little areas as if they were vital, exquisite points of detail, but I could see the whole thing was actually just a mess.

This was right at the beginning of the first term, before we'd even met the other students and tutors. In fact, we were both here a day early; most of our peers wouldn't be here until tomorrow. I couldn't wait to get started. I had come to check out the art block, to see if I could meet any of the tutors and find out what this uni-lark was going to be like, and I presumed he'd had the same idea. However, the reality was that he'd come here to draw, to express, to vent. It's how he got through the days.

"Hello," I said, but he didn't hear me. I noticed the white earphone wires which disappeared inside his hood, so I stepped closer to him, standing beside him, waiting for him to notice me. It didn't occur to me that I shouldn't intrude upon his reverie. I just thought he was probably as keen to meet the other students as I was. I crouched down beside him, and watched him for a while, not sure whether he knew I was there. At last, he stopped his iPod, removed his earphones, and turned his bright blue eyes on me.

"Alright?" I said, and smiled. He nodded uncertainly. "I'm Matthew," I said. "Matt," I elaborated, and put out my hand. He looked at it as if he didn't know what it was, then got the idea and shook it with his own clammy, charcoal-encrusted hand.

"I'm Marcus," he said. "Sorry for ignoring you," he went on, revealing a slight West Country accent and a surprisingly soft voice.

"Who you listening to?" I said, thinking he looked as if he might like the same bands as me.

"Oh," he said, taking a moment to realise what I meant. "Steinbeck," he said. I looked blankly at him: not a band I'd heard of. "*The Grapes of Wrath*," he added. Seeing my confusion, he clarified: "It's a book."

"Oh," I grinned, surprised. "I've never ..."

"It's very long and incredibly dull," he said, returning my smile and looking a little sheepish. "I just like it cos ... Oh, well, it's really sad," he finished quickly, imagining he was boring me. He wasn't, and I questioned him about it. His eyes were wide and passionate, yet the whole time he kept his hood up as if he were peering out of a cave, fearful of the world beyond. And as he told me how *The Grapes of Wrath* moved him so deeply, I became aware that I should ask him about his picture. I confess I wasn't really listening to what he was saying; I had no interest in Steinbeck, in fact I really wasn't a reader at all. But I liked having him open up to me, and I enjoyed his gentle, tentative excitement. As he spoke I studied his picture and tried to think of something to say about it: abstract art was so out of my field of understanding, but, although I didn't really like this piece, I did like this artist, and was eager to keep him talking. And suddenly I saw it: right there in the middle of the picture– no, not in the middle, that would be too balanced. It was a little to one side and a little high: a figure, twisted and wracked by some unknown pain, almost invisible amongst the swirls and smudges, but depicted in subtle detail, beautifully rendered. Male or female you could not tell, but once you'd seen it you couldn't understand how you'd missed it. Marcus had a talent, and I was excited to have met him.

He also had a teddy bear. I hadn't noticed it at first; the room was cluttered with all sorts of artifacts, presumably accumulated to play their part in endless still life compositions over the years, but the grubby, threadbare teddy on the floor turned out to be his.

"Uh, mind Jeremy," he said to me as I adjusted myself to a more comfortable sitting position, accidentally catching the thing with my foot.

"Sorry?" I said, unsure whether or not he was joking.

He moved the bear to the other side of him, and looked away as if he'd said too much. "Is it yours?" I said.

"*He,*" he corrected me.

111

"Hello Jeremy!" I said after a long few seconds of silence. Marcus looked at me, assessing whether or not he thought I was taking the piss. I smiled, and he seem to accept that I wasn't.

To break the awkwardness of the moment, I was about to tell him how great I thought his picture was, but he leapt up suddenly, Jeremy in the crook of his arm, and said, "We should go to the bar! I've never seen such cheap beer. Come on, Jeremy's buying!"

*

As it happened, Jeremy wasn't buying at all. Neither was Marcus, but I didn't mind. I had no concept of the value of money at that point, and with my dependable weekly allowance from my comfortably middle class parents I thought nothing of funding a night of drinking for the three of us—yes, Jeremy needed a drink too, but only a half, and that did last him all night.

There was a small group of students there too, already half-cut judging by the noise they were making. I sensed Marcus' reticence to sit near them, so we found a table in a recess at the other end of the bar. Marcus rolled himself a spliff, and I was in awe at his audacity. This was well before the smoking ban, but a spliff! I was a pretty liberal guy who considered myself a man of the world. I'd been stoned before, but never so brazenly as this. I think people thought I was quite cool, but I found myself looking up to my new friend, wowed by his total disregard for the rules, as well as by his artistic talents and his strange, appealing manner. He looked like someone who needed protecting. He wasn't smoking a spliff to be cool, he was smoking it to soothe his inner pain. He was the enigmatically tortured figure that stable, grounded people like me idolise. And those pretty eyes of his ...

I don't think I was trying to chat him up. That was never my way. If something was going to happen, it would happen; I wouldn't force it. Besides, everything was new and exciting. I knew there would be all sorts of doorways opening for me over the coming weeks and years, and, I knew - somewhat arrogantly - many of them would be of the bedroom variety. I was in no rush. I didn't even know for sure that Marcus was openly gay, although I was pretty sure he could be swayed.

We talked, and laughed, and got slightly stoned. Marcus didn't push his luck too much; one spliff was enough for now, though after that he did smoke Marlboros like there was no tomorrow, and we drank lager. I was still at that stage of trying to force myself to like it, and suppressed a shudder after every gulp.

"God, I hate this stuff," I laughed, but Marcus just said, "Yeah but it's cheap." He seemed to relish it.

I suppose we didn't get half as drunk that night as we did on many occasions later on, but it still felt exciting and daring and new and mature. At last, we decided to head back to halls. Marcus scooped up Jeremy, who was the only one not giddy with mirth and joy, and we headed for the exit, just as the other bunch of students was leaving too. There were only five of them. I later learned that they were a mixture of P.E., Science and Maths students, and they didn't remain friends very long into the term. But tonight, they were all buddies together, all pepped up on hope and glory, and Kronenberg.

"Woah!" one of them said to us just as we reached the

exit. "What, not going to introduce yourselves?" He was big and beefy, and drunk.

"Yeah," said another. "Come on, don't be shy." He was the one who turned out to be a maths student, and he fitted the stereotype in every way: glasses, side parting, spots.

I stopped and smiled, and Marcus put his hood up.

"I'm Matt," I said, "And this is Marcus."

"I'm Pete," the beefy guy said, "but everyone calls me Captain."

"Good to meet you, Pete," I said, inwardly vowing never to call him Captain. Looking back, it's incredible how we all adhered so rigidly to our stereotypes: maths student; P.E. student; art student. And all the while, Marcus was clearing his throat theatrically. At last, that filtered through to my consciousness and I glanced at him. He was urging me, with his big eyes, to mention his teddy bear.

"Oh yes," I said, "and this is Jeremy." There was a brief pause in proceedings, followed by laughter. They were as confused as I'd been that first moment after Marcus had shown me Jeremy. Was he joking? Was he mocking them somehow? That's what they were all thinking. I knew Marcus wasn't doing any of those things, but I saw how delicate the situation had become.

"Jeremy's very tired and ready for bed," Marcus said quietly, to me, withdrawing into his hood again like a frightened tortoise.

"He's what?" said Pete.

"You are joking, right?" said the maths student, squinting squiffily through his glasses. There were comments from some of the others too, all high on comradeship and first-day bravado.

"Come on mate," Pete said. "You're a big boy now. Put the teddy away."

At this, Marcus gave the campest wince you could possibly imagine. Even *I* hadn't seen how effeminate he could be until that moment. "How rude!" he wailed, an expression of horror on his face. He consoled poor Jeremy with a heartfelt, and wholly provocative, cuddle.

"You big gay," Pete said, disgusted. "You're away from Mummy and Daddy now. Time to forget your teddy bear and act like a grown up."

"Don't you listen, Jeremy," Marcus said, covering the bear's ears. "Nasty Pete's just jealous because his teddy bear's got glasses and spots." And he shoved his way past them and flounced out into the night.

To my surprise and relief, Pete, the affronted maths student and the others let him go, with just a few more shouts of "Gay!" Later on, once Pete had been joined by other, like-minded students, and felt a bit more comfortable in this new world, he actually turned out to be not too bad, though this would not be the last time he'd clash with Marcus.

That night, Marcus and I just laughed. "Gay!" I teased him as we giggled and guffawed our way back through the car park towards our block. "You gay," he teased me back. It turned out we were both in the same block, although on different floors, but it wasn't until a few months later that anything happened between us. That night, we were both just happy to have found a friend.

*

I realise now that I never properly knew Marcus. I mean, I *knew* him outwardly: we were great friends and, eventually, partners; I understood *how* he ticked, but I never knew *why* he ticked that way. I loved his strange, incongruous combination of tenderness, passion, weakness and strength. He came across as deeply shy, but had moments of flamboyant gregariousness. He was weak and needy, but could be bold and self-assured too, like the way he smoked spliffs so openly in public, and the way he could, at times, stand up for himself. I could see he was full of emotional pain, but that just fascinated me. I never tried to unravel it.

Later on, that first Autumn, he and I were kicking our way through damp leaves on the way to the library, when we encountered Pete, who by now had shed the spotty maths student and acquired a band of sporty disciples. Funnily enough, I never suffered for being friends with a weirdo like Marcus; whenever I met these guys on my own, there was no problem between us. I was like that, as I said before: uninhibited, relaxed, and that seemed to make me likeable. I even played a few games of tennis with Pete, and never once did I call him Captain.

But here he was now with his mates. They'd clearly done a bit of afternoon drinking, and were in mischievous spirits.

"Isn't that your boyfriend, Captain?" I heard one of the lads say as they approached us.

"Hello ladies," Pete greeted us, ignoring the comment. Marcus, holding Jeremy under one arm as usual, tugged at the drawstring which tightened his hood around his face.

"Alright, Pete," I said, grinning at the way they were all swaying.

"How's it going?" Pete asked me, his eyes slightly glazed. So far, he was ignoring Marcus.

"Not bad," I said. "You've been in the bar then?"

"Pufters," one of the other lads hissed under a pretend clear of the throat.

"It's only me who's the pufter actually," I said, deciding it was best to brazen it out. I'd made no secret of my sexuality, and this was before Marcus had officially come out.

"I'm not so sure about that," said a tall guy named Freddie, and winked at Marcus. The lads were laughing and chipping in with their own garbled comments and sound effects now.

"Are you alright in there, funny little weird guy?" Pete said to Marcus. He was taking the piss, but he did that to everyone. Despite his attitude on our first encounter with him, there was no real malice in him, but I knew his attention would make Marcus deeply uncomfortable. "You fascinate me," Pete said. "What is going on in that weird little head?" and he pressed his index finger against Marcus' hooded cranium.

"He's got a teddy bear," the tall guy stated the blindingly obvious.

"Oh well done Miss Marple!" Pete chided him. "He's right though, Matty," Pete informed me. "Your bum chum has got a teddy bear."

"'Bum chum'?" I retorted, amused. "Seriously? You're really going to use that term?"

"Alright, 'rent boy' then," he said, shoving me hard in the chest so I staggered backwards. The lads laughed. It was harmless banter, but I knew Marcus didn't like it. "He looks happy though," Pete said with deliberate irony:

117

Marcus never looked happy when there were other people around.

"Looks rancid, that bear," the tall guy said. "I'll bet it stinks!" The comment drew laughter and more jibes from the other lads.

Marcus whispered something into Jeremy's fraying ear. Then, out loud he said: "I don't think it's nice, you laughing." The lads went quiet, partly through surprise and partly because they were straining to hear him. "I don't think it's nice you laughing," Marcus said again. I knew he was quoting Clint Eastwood, but he made no effort whatsoever to not sound camp. "You see, Jeremy here gets the crazy idea you're laughing at him. Now if you'll apologise like I know you're gonna, I might convince him you didn't mean it."

"Bloody 'ell, Captain, it's Bruce Willis," one of them laughed.

"It's Charles Bronson," someone else wrongly corrected him. "Isn't it?"

"I'm waiting," Marcus said, his eyes locked on the tall guy.

"What for?"

"Your apology." Sometimes, I did wish Marcus could just let things drop. These lads were laughing at him.

"I'm not apologising to you, dickhead."

Marcus seemed to accept that, but added quietly, "You will."

Pete slapped the back of his hand against the tall guy's chest. "Be nice, Freddie," he said. Then, to us, he announced: "We're going to crack open a bottle of tequila, do some slammers. You gaylords coming?"

"No thanks," Marcus said quietly.

"Another time, Pete," I quickly interjected. "You chaps knock yerselves out though!"

"Come on, Captain," Freddie said. "Let's go. I'm gagging for one."

"Ooh, gay," someone else chided.

"See you later then, gays," Pete concluded. But then he snatched Jeremy, eliciting a great shriek from Marcus, and chucked him at Freddie who caught him and bolted out of reach of Marcus' wildly flailing arms. Marcus was uncoordinated at the best of times, and this reaction did not exactly endear him to a gang of sporty lads. Pete and Freddie headed off across the grounds between shrubberies and bike sheds, passing poor Jeremy back and forth between them like a rugby ball, and soon the others had joined them. Freddy turned and goaded Marcus, sniffing Jeremy and calling out, "Woah! I was right! It fuckin' stinks!" Marcus, having abandoned his dignity entirely, gave chase, and I jogged along behind, wondering how to diffuse the situation. Pete had reached his block now, and the lads all followed him raucously inside, Jeremy and all. Marcus looked at me, helpless and distraught. I patted his shoulder and told him not to worry. A few moments later, Jeremy appeared at a second floor window, held outside briefly by a long, muscular arm, before disappearing back inside. Then came the sound of thumping music.

"They're only trying to get a reaction out of you," I said, seeing Marcus' expression of fury. "Just leave it. You'll get Jeremy back tomorrow."

"No," Marcus snapped. "I'm not leaving him alone with those bastards. I have to help him." He yanked open the door and went into the block. I followed. He was heading up the stairs, talking to himself and adjusting his hood around his face as if he was a scientist entering an infected zone. I could barely keep up with him as he strode up two flights of stairs on those long thin legs, and then went through the door into the second floor corridor. He stopped, looked at the fire extinguisher on the wall, and lifted it carefully from its hook.

"Christ Marcus, what you gonna do with that?" I asked.

"Just watch," he said grimly.

"Marcus, you do know Jeremy is just a teddy bear, don't you? You can live without him." But he just shot me a filthy look, and marched off along the landing. There was no problem locating the right room: the door was wide open and the music was filling the corridor. Marcus pulled the yellow safety pin from the extinguisher and walked straight in.

"Jeremy?" he called over the music's thumping energy. "There you are!" I was behind him, struggling to see what was going on.

"Are you joking?" I heard one of Pete's mates say.

"No. Give me Jeremy or this thing goes off," Marcus said, giving the nozzle of the extinguisher an assertive jerk. As I squeezed round him I saw he was pointing it straight at Pete's laptop which was open and on, providing the music via a huge set of speakers. "First the laptop, then the speakers," Marcus said. The lads were all lolling on beanbags, Pete's bed and the floor, about six of them, and some were grinning at this lunacy, but some were looking uncertain. Pete leaned forwards, his hands out defensively. Beside him, Freddie sat, mouth slightly open, visibly amused.

"You know I will kill you if wreck my laptop," Pete

warned over the pounding of the music.

"Give me Jeremy then," reasoned Marcus. I could see Jeremy now, on the windowsill. Someone had put a pair of sunglasses on him and sellotaped a cigarette to his paw.

"I think Jeremy likes it here," said Freddie. "He needs a father figure in his life."

"Shut up," Pete said, seeing the danger his computer was in. "Give him the teddy."

Someone obediently held Jeremy towards Marcus, who in turn nodded towards me and I took him. I removed the cigarette and shades and put them on the side.

But Marcus was still not relenting. The extinguisher's nozzle hovering dangerously over the laptop, he looked now at Freddie and said, "I'll have that apology now please."

"What? You gotta be kidding."

"You either apologise to me now, or you apologise to Pete in a couple of minutes time when you're wringing the water out of his laptop for him."

Freddie glanced at Pete, and back at Marcus. I chipped in, "I really don't think he's kidding, Freddie."

"Alright mate, I'm sorry. Christ, get some perspective!"

"You need counselling or something mate," Pete informed Marcus, acidly. "I should have burnt that stupid bear; I'd be doing you a favour." Marcus looked at him with utter hatred. I was convinced he was about to soak the laptop this time, and I put my hand on his arm to calm him. He shook me away and stepped towards Pete, the others in the room loving the show, laughing behind hands as the dance music thumped excitedly. Pete looked unsettled, shifted in his beanbag. Marcus bent, holding the extinguisher's nozzle towards Pete, bringing it slowly closer and closer until he literally inserted it into the nervous but unflinching Pete's right nostril. Pete glared back at him, slapped his broad hand round Marcus' skinny wrist, and we all held our breath.

Then, Marcus stepped away and Pete released his wrist. Marcus backed towards the door like a cowboy who had narrowly averted a gunfight in a saloon, and I wanted to laugh. Pete's mates were grinning in a mixture of sadistic joy at Pete's humiliation, and admiration for Marcus. I waved Jeremy at them, and we were back out in the corridor. Raucous laughter erupted in the room behind us as we walked calmly away.

That was the night Marcus and I properly got together. It happened almost by accident. He came back to my room, we put some music on, got stoned, and laughed together until about two in the morning. We were both sitting on the bed, slowly sinking into pillows and cushions, Jeremy propped between us. Marcus made no move to leave, and I wondered if he was wanting what I was wanting. I had no way of knowing. At some point, he began to doze, and slumped against my legs. I stroked his hair, and whispered, "You can stay if you like." He did, but only because he was too stoned to walk back up to his own room. Well, that was his excuse anyway. Drowsy, we stripped down to our underwear, and slid into bed. We spooned. Well, I spooned him, and he held Jeremy. Marcus was out for the count at this point, and I didn't even know if he was aware I was there. I slept, but only a little. Despite the loveliness of being so close to an almost naked Marcus, I was really uncomfortable. But, at last, sunlight woke us. He groaned, and shifted, and I thought he was going to get up, and the bubble would be broken. I put my hand on his arm, and gently urged him to stay. It was a bold move, and it could have been a disastrous one; Marcus had always told me he wasn't gay, but I had never really believed him.

"Did you sleep okay?" I whispered, my lips close to his hair. There was a silence, and I thought I'd blown it. I thought he was going to get all awkward, and leave, and that would be our friendship ruined. My hand was still on his warm arm and I knew I should just let him go, but I didn't. I gently squeezed his muscle, and stroked him with my thumb. He turned. The bed bounced and I felt his knees and toenails against my legs and feet. He must have put Jeremy down on the floor because there was nothing between us now except the warmth of the bed. I shifted a little closer, so that his nose was only a centimetre or two from mine, and we could smell each other's morning breath, but neither of us cared. I could feel something else too: straining at the fabric of his boxers, his morning hard-on brushed briefly against mine. I moved my hand slowly down his arm, and I saw fear in his eyes. "It's okay," I said, tentatively stroking my fingers further down, to his elbow, and then his hip. I smiled. And he smiled too. And that was how it all began.

*

I look back on that time in my life with intense, angry, clawing regret. I don't mean I regret sleeping with Marcus; I don't regret that at all. But I regret the way I failed him. He needed help, and I could have provided it. I should have questioned him about his past. I found his eccentricity deeply endearing, but where had it come

123

from? He was obsessively attached to Jeremy, and I wish I'd asked why. I know the truth now of course, but if I'd known it *then,* I could have been helping him, instead of just ... *enjoying* him.

There was, following the fire extinguisher incident, a period of peace between Marcus and the others, partly because their paths so rarely crossed. Marcus didn't bear grudges once he'd got the better of someone, and so he didn't mind that I joined Pete and Freddie and the other lads for games of tennis and badminton, and occasionally made the numbers up in non-tournament footy matches. The lads ribbed me mercilessly about my sexuality, but I knew they weren't really bothered anymore; uni life has a way of mellowing people; and I talked openly and matter-of-factly about it. Sometimes they asked me deeply personal questions about mine and Marcus' sex life, and I answered them brazenly with the most shockingly depraved and graphic exaggerations I could muster. They knew I was making most of it up; we were all just having a laugh.

Once Marcus and I had got together, he didn't seem bothered about hiding it. I'd expected him to struggle with the whole coming-out thing, but to be fair to him, he just, sort of, followed my lead. People had been accusing him of being gay for years, and he'd been transparently denying it, both to himself and to others. I think that once he could no longer deny it to himself, he just got on with it, perhaps relieved that at least this part of his life was now under a sort of control.

Or at least, that's how I saw it at the time. What I didn't realise was that he was living with despair on so many levels, and it wasn't the love I provided which helped keep it at bay, it was, at first, cannabis, then other, harder drugs. This was uni; we both dabbled. But he dabbled deeper than I realised. We didn't live in each other's pockets; in fact sometimes whole days and nights went by without me seeing Marcus at all. He often didn't want to come into town with me and other friends I'd made, but he didn't mind me going. Then, one night at around three a.m., I returned to halls, let myself into his room as I often did, and found him lying in his boxers, outstretched across his rug, a syringe lying near his open, upturned palm.

For a moment, I really thought he was dead, but no, he was lost in an unconscious ecstasy far greater, far more all-consuming, than all of the love, support, friendship and sex that I could ever provide. I was heartbroken.

*

I will carry the burden of horrible shame with me 'til the day I die, but I abandoned Marcus after that. We saw each other every day in the art block, and around the campus, but Marcus was shrinking into himself, and I just wanted to have fun. I was appalled and hurt that he'd turned to drugs when he'd had me there to help him. Was my love not enough? He'd rather have the false, brief kicks those dealer friends of his could provide; people who didn't care if he lived or died. How disgusting of me to interpret Marcus' turmoil as a personal insult against me. I don't think we ever officially split up, but over the course of a term or two, and the separation of a summer holidays, we ceased to be a couple. It was as if we'd accidentally got on two different trains and were gazing at each other as the trains pulled away in opposite directions.

*

Some way through the Summer term, Marcus stopped turning up for lectures. I felt no guilt; I had no concept at that time of my own failings, but, on a selfish level, I missed him, and I was worried about him too. Even though we weren't together anymore, even though I had started to make the most of being single and free and quite good looking, I missed him. There were other boys in my life now, but none who made me feel the way Marcus once had.

I knocked on his door late one afternoon. I didn't let myself in anymore, although I still had his spare key in my pocket. Who knows, he could be with someone else. How would I feel then?

"Yep," he called, which I knew meant 'come in'. I did. He was sitting cross-legged on his bed working on some new work of art. His hair was thick and wild. His grey t-shirt looked as if he'd been using it as a cleaning cloth, and his skinny, white knee peered at me through the obligatory rip in the black denim of his jeans.

"Alright?" he said, looking genuinely pleased to see me.

"Hello mate," I said. "Not seen you for a few days. You alright?"

He took a long draw on a fat spliff and grinned, "Peachy." I saw now that he was working on a huge collage: a messy miscellany of ripped up magazine pages, torn strips of fabric, and other, more solid objects, glued, nailed and stapled to a wooden board. As usual, there was a figure in amongst the maelstrom, this time depicted in a

126

single black outline made of wool.

I peered at it, closing the door behind me. "Spilt your bin?" I said.

"Hilarious, Matt," he said with a brief, fake smile. The room stank: a heady mix of cannabis, smoke, dirty laundry and scented candles.

"You okay?" I said. "You weren't in lectures today."

Now peering over his collage, looking for somewhere to place the fragment of cloth in his careful fingers, he mock-cleared his throat pointedly, as if to remind me something.

"Hello Jeremy," I said, knowing I'd not get any sense out of Marcus until I'd at least acknowledged the grubby bear, propped beside him as if learning how to collage.

Marcus gave a nod of acceptance and said, "Jeremy has missed you."

"I've missed you too," I said, not specifically to the bear. I slumped into the rotten-looking beanbag, sending a puff of polystyrene balls out of its side. "You weren't in any lectures today," I repeated.

"I'm never in lectures," he shrugged, not looking up. "Hadn't you noticed?"

"Well, yes, I had," I said. "I've been worried."

"Have you?" He paused in his work just for an instant, but he didn't look at me.

"'Course I was."

"It's alright you know," he said. "I'm not a drug addict. I don't need you to look after me." He wasn't cross; his tone was gentle and reassuring.

"I know. You *want* me to though, eh?" I said, with what I judged to be a cheeky smirk. Briefly, he peered at me through his ragged fringe with smiling eyes.

"Are you flirting?" he said, eyes on his collage again.
"Maybe."

*

That night, we went into town, mates, not partners, but at least we were friends. We spent several hours in a gay bar where I had to nurse Jeremy and watch as Marcus snogged three different guys and danced his weird, snaky dance with several others. This was one of his 'gregarious' nights, when his shyness and anxieties seemed to let go of him, releasing him to soar and fly wherever the mood took him. He'd be back into his shell by morning, but it was great to see him like this, even if I was burning with jealousy.

But things took a different turn on the way home.

"Alright gays?" came Pete's too-loud drawl as we made our way along the high street, arm in arm. I was practically holding Marcus up; he'd been on the tequilas, a tipple he wasn't used to. My heart sank. I really didn't want Pete invading our weird bubble. But there was no stopping him. Suddenly, he was draping his heavy self over both of us, which nearly brought Marcus to the floor. I shoved Pete off, really hard. You had to be like that with Pete, but he didn't seem to mind. In fact, he hardly noticed. The other lads were behind him, not paying much attention to us. "Where've you been?" Pete drawled. "Out gaying?"

"Gaying?" I said, vaguely amused. "Yep, you should've come with us Pete. Right up your alley."

"Fuck off out of my alley!" Pete laughed drunkenly. "Getting the bus back then?"

"Yeah, probably."

"Is he alright?" Pete said, throwing his arm around Marcus so hard he wrenched him away from me.

"Never knew you cared," I said.

"Of course I care," he scowled in mock hurt. "You alright little fella?" he said, his finger pulling at the edge of Marcus' hood.

"Yep," Marcus said. "Are you?"

"Wahoo, it speaks!" Pete shrieked. "Come on, let's get you home."

Between us, we got Marcus onto the bus. For some reason we saw fit to make things really hard for ourselves and drag him all the way to the top deck. After a rowdy journey where Pete's mates regaled everyone with bawdy jokes and exaggerated tales of their own sexual prowess, peppered with inventive swears and a couple of vomits, we were soon guiding Marcus back through the campus towards halls. That was when I suddenly realised something.

"Shit," I said, and immediately wished I hadn't.

"What?" Marcus and Pete said simultaneously.

"Oh, nothing," I said, looking over Marcus' head straight at Pete, warning him with my eyes not to pursue it. But he didn't have to.

"Where's Jeremy?" Marcus said, stopping.

"Ah, he's ..." I said, desperately looking at Pete for help.

"He's on the fuckin' bus!" Marcus said. The effect of the realisation was like a dose of smelling salts. He shook me off him and headed back towards the road. It was beginning to rain. Pete's mates, who'd been following close behind us, parted like the Red Sea as Marcus marched straight through them.

"Marcus!" I shouted, chasing. "Wait, you can't go looking for him like this." As if to prove my point, Marcus suddenly veered sideways into a flower bed. I got to him just as he was struggling to his feet, half filthy. I steadied him, but he lurched off again.

"I have to save him," he said. I knew it was too late, the bus was long gone. Maybe we could phone the bus company in the morning. For someone who, a few moments ago, had been barely able to walk, Marcus was moving impressively quickly now. But soon he had forgotten which way horizontal went, and was tilting sideways into the ground again. I reached him in time to stop him really hurting himself, but it was then I realised he was crying real tears. "I have to save him," he slurred. "I've got to save him." I don't think I had ever really known what people mean when they say 'it broke my heart', but at that moment, I had a pain of love and sympathy in my chest so intense I almost choked. I even imagined poor Jeremy alone on the bus, wondering why Marcus had abandoned him. I wrapped my arms around Marcus and held him to me, partly to stop him getting up again, and partly to soothe his sorrow.

"Is he alright?" Pete said, arriving beside me, wet from the drizzle I'd hardly noticed. He sounded genuinely concerned.

"No, I'm not alright," Marcus suddenly shouted, his mouth all salivary, like a tantruming child. "I've got to save Jeremy."

"We'll find him, mate," Pete said. "Don't worry."

"He's right," I said. "We'll phone the bus company in the morn—"

"I need to help him now," Marcus shrieked. He

sounded totally out of control. "I need to save him!"

"Marcus," I said, "you can't. Not now. You have to let him go. We'll save him, but you have to wait now, until tomorrow."

I felt him go limp. As if he'd just shut down. To Pete's credit, he never once said what I was thinking, which was: *It's only a teddy bear.*

Between us, we helped Marcus up, and half carried, half dragged him back to his room. Pete's mates had dispersed into the campus, and I was grateful to Pete for helping me out. I really don't think I could have got Marcus back without him. He left us then, and at last I was on my own with Marcus. It was funny, I'd never seen him without Jeremy. I'd always thought the bear was a comical prop, an affectation, but I could see now that Jeremy really meant a lot to him. I hugged Marcus, helped him get his wet jacket off. He was filthy down one side, and I did my best to clean him up before I let him get into bed. All the time he was muttering, "I couldn't save him. I couldn't save him."

I watched him slip into a drunken sleep. And I knew what I had to do.

Once I was satisfied he was dead to the world, I put my coat back on and slipped out into the rain. It was gone four o'clock in the morning and it was pouring down now.

I ran back towards the town centre, going against the direction of the bus route. I was hoping I'd see the bus coming towards me, jump on it, find Jeremy, and ride the bus back to halls for my hero's welcome. But I had practically got all the way back into town before I saw one. It was a night bus now of course, but it had the right number on the front so I knew it was possibly the same bus. I climbed, weary and wet, to the top deck. The smell of sick told me it probably was the same bus, so I searched the seats where we'd been. And the seats where we hadn't been. And the floor. And the lower deck too.

Jeremy was not there.

The sky was beginning to lighten as I made my way back up the path to halls. I decided not to go to Marcus' room. He was spark out, and I didn't want to admit my failure when he woke. I slept 'til about ten, when I was woken by someone knocking on my door. "Come in," I called croakily.

"It's Freddie," came the answer from the other side.

"I said come in. It's not locked." The door opened slowly, and Freddie appeared, looking sheepish. In his hand was Jeremy.

"Sorry, mate," he said, waggling the bear slightly. "Just thought it was a bit of fun. Didn't know Marcus would get so ... you know." I just looked at him. "Captain said I shouldn't have ... Anyway, here he is. *It*. Here *it* is I should say," and he gave an uncomfortable snigger at his slip. He placed Jeremy on my desk, and stood there looking at me, smiling awkwardly.

"What do you want? A cup of tea?" I said.

"Oh, yeah okay," he brightened.

"Fuck off you prick," I said angrily. Freddie realised I meant it and left.

I got up, dressed, and picked Jeremy up. I looked at that slightly rancid, smelly, frayed bear and wondered why on earth Marcus was so besotted with him. Still, at least he was back now, so I went up to return him to Marcus. Maybe I'd get that hero's welcome after all.

I knocked on his door, Jeremy playfully placed just

inside my jumper, peering out of the neck.

No answer.

I knocked again, then wondered why I was knocking. Surely we were back on letting-ourselves-into-each-other's-rooms terms now. I put my hand on the handle, but found the door was locked. Ah, he must have gone out. He wouldn't have locked it if he was in there. I had his spare key in my jeans pocket. I could let myself in and put Jeremy in his bed! If I played it right, I might even manage to be with Marcus when he came back and discovered what I'd done!

I unlocked the door, opened it tentatively, suddenly anxious that Marcus might appear in the corridor and catch me at it, and I crept inside.

My world turned blood red.

Marcus was on the floor, on his back, syringe still stuck in his arm. His mouth was full of foam and his eyes were half open.

*

Marcus' death utterly disassembled me. It was as if my whole being had flown apart into a million tiny bits. I had loved him, and his loss was too much to bear. But more than that, I had never before known that emotional pain can be passed from person to person, like a contagion, mutating as it spreads: hatred in one person creating, through the events it controls, fear or sadness in another and guilt in someone else. That's why, after a little more than a year, I returned to uni, but now with a new sense of purpose. I switched courses, and began a journey which led to a career as a child psychologist. Marcus' pain had infected me in ways I still can barely comprehend, or live with, but I have dedicated my life to stopping others from spreading theirs.

His parents were a kind, gentle, middle aged couple. At the funeral, I'd hardly spoken to them. I could hardly speak to anyone. And, probably, neither could they. But I decided to pay them a visit, once the horror of Marcus' death had settled into a steady, deep agony which I could hide but couldn't shift.

There was no reason for them to welcome me in. They didn't know anything about me. They didn't know whether I'd been his friend or one of the ones who had made his life difficult. They presumably didn't know he was gay, and so they *couldn't* know how close Marcus and I had been, and I couldn't tell them. But they *did* welcome me in, and they talked very openly about Marcus.

They'd adopted him when he was six. Fostered him first. His real parents had abused him horribly. But worse than that, Marcus had had to watch the terrible things they did to his younger brother. The things those pretty blue eyes of his had seen ... I imagined Marcus as a child, helplessly watching them hurt his tiny brother; hearing the screaming; unable to stop them; unable to save him, until, unnoticed by the outside world, the poor little boy had died. And of course, he was called Jeremy.

Me and Robbie

I love my Robbie. He's so brave. I'll tell you about the brave thing he did and what happened next, and what happened after that too.

We was walking past Kentucky Fried Chicken when we saw that boy who lives above us. He was a nasty piece of work, you could tell. He'd only lived there a few days. He always got his hood up, and always looked like he'd been in a fight, and he got things tattooed on his knuckles. Words. I didn't know what they said, I never got close enough to read them. I'm not very good at reading anyway. I'm better than my Robbie though. But that's okay because he's the brave one.

The boy, the one with the hood and the tattoos, he never liked us. He always looked at us as if we smell bad. We don't; we always wash and shower just like we were taught. Just because we got learning difficulties doesn't mean we don't know how to keep clean. That boy, he looked at us as if we're horrible, Robbie and me. He's not the only one, lots of people did that. They always do. My mum tells me to ignore people like that. They may be able to read better than me and Robbie, but we're better than those people. That's what Liz Jones says too. But it makes me cross when those people are nasty to us, because my Robbie's so kind. No-one should think he's a horrible person. I can be annoying, I know that, because I'm always giggling for no reason, and I sulk a lot too, and have tantrums. Robbie's just quiet and kind, and that's why I love him.

Anyway, there's another way you could tell that boy with the hood was nasty. He was horrible to his dog. It was a cute, brown one that looked strong and gentle, but my mum and Liz Jones said it was one of those dangerous dogs. I don't think it was dangerous though. It always looked scared. It flinched when the boy shouted at it. And it got scars. That made me and Robbie hate that boy because we both love dogs, especially Robbie does.

When we went past the Kentucky we saw that boy and his dog. He was with his friends. They all looked as nasty as he was. They always laughed when they saw us coming. That makes me really cross. It's not Robbie's fault he walks funny. But that day, Robbie and me saw that boy drop half a Kentucky Fried Chicken on the pavement outside for his dog to eat. He didn't care about that dog. He should have given it dog food, not Kentucky Fried Chicken. And he said, "Eat it," like that, angry and mean. And the dog did, but it looked like it didn't want to, as if it knowed it shouldn't. And my Robbie said, "You shouldn't give that to a dog," but Robbie's got a quiet voice, and he always looks at the floor and people can't always tell what he's saying. The boy said, "What?" like that, cross. And his friends started to laugh and say things about us. I can't remember what, but not nice things. "Chicken bones are bad for dogs," Robbie said. I was proud of Robbie then because it was like he wasn't scared of the boy even though he looked so rough and nasty and all his friends were there. The boy said, "You'd know, Brain of Britain," and his friend said, "Can't you give her chicken then?" pointing to me. I knowed what he meant. He meant I was a dog, which is rude. And another boy said, "Can't you give your girlfriend your bone?" and they all laughed at that a lot.

Me and Robbie kept on walking. I was holding Robbie's arm which made me feel safe. Robbie was looking at the pavement and saying things even I couldn't tell what they were. When we'd gone quite far, Robbie said, "I hate them." I knew what he meant. He hated them for being horrible to the dog. He said, "I'm going to buy that dog off him." I was excited. I love dogs and always wanted one. I started laughing and pulling on his arm but he just kept walking and saying things I couldn't hear properly. The cash machine was miles away and Robbie got out some money and then we went all the way back again to the Kentucky. But the boys were all gone. I sulked because I wanted us to have that dog.

When we were back home I kept thinking about that dog. I wanted to rescue it. That night we heard a horrible row coming from upstairs. That's where the boy lived. There was a lady there too. They always rowed. It was horrible to hear it. We thinked he hit her sometimes. Quite a lot actually. We could always hear them shouting at each other and screaming at each other, and the dog would bark at them. But sometimes you'd hear the poor dog yelp as if someone had hurted it. I said, "That nasty boy, he's hitting his wife, and the dog gets stuck in to help her, and then he kicks it or something." Me and my Robbie just cuddled. We didn't know what to do. They'd only lived there a week or two, but they were spoiling our happy home.

We loved our home, our little flat. We'd maked it all pretty by painting the walls and putting up pictures.

People used to think we couldn't do it but we did, and I'm glad they used to think that because it maked it seem so exciting and nice when we did do it. We could say, "There. We done it. Told you we could." And we were really happy there. And my mum helped us, and Liz Jones, always came round to make sure we were doing okay. She was nice. But that boy living upstairs spoilt everything a bit. Me and Robbie felt sad listening to the poor dog getting hurt.

It was really bad that night. You could hear things breaking and the dog was barking like mad. Me and Robbie knowed the boy was going to hurt it if it didn't stop barking. Robbie said, "We should do something." He was right, we both knowed it but we couldn't think what to do. I said Mum had always said to ring her if we didn't know what to do about something, and Robbie said, "She's out."

"How do you know that?" I said.

"She told us that," Robbie said. "She told us on the 14th of March." Robbie always remembers things like that, he does. Then he started telling me exactly what we were doing on the 14th of March, and I listened because the 14th of March was a nice day when we met my mum and Liz Jones in the park and had a nice walk and Liz Jones said it was the warmest day of the year so far. But the shouting and barking from upstairs maded us remember the poor dog and the lady too. "I'm going to phone my mum," I said, and Robbie said, "I just told you, she's out."

"Oh yes," I said. Then I decided to call Liz Jones instead. I rang her number, but I was embarrassed so I threw the phone to Robbie and I started to giggle for no reason. It wasn't funny, I was scared, so I don't know why I giggled. But Robbie isn't very good talking on the phone and he mumbled some things slowly. Even I couldn't really tell what he was saying. I was cross with him, and I taked the phone off him. I said, "Liz Jones, it's Eleanor and Robbie. We're scared and we don't know what to do. The man upstairs is hurting his wife and his dog and we want to make it stop. Listen," I said and I holded the phone up so she could hear the row. "Can you come and make them stop?" Liz Jones didn't say anything, and I waited but she still didn't say anything, and then there was a beep. It was an answering machine. "Why didn't you tell me it was an answering machine?" I said to Robbie, and Robbie said he did, but he didn't.

"Stay here," Robbie told me.

"Where are you going?" I said. I was scared and I felt sick. I wanted to be near my Robbie.

"I'm going to look," he said.

"To look where?" I said, but Robbie was already putting his shoes on. I tied up the laces for him and then I did mine. I had to tell him to wait, and he would have gone out of the door by himself if I hadn't grabbed his coat with my teeth while I tied up my laces. Then I went with him, holding his arm. I love Robbie's arms, they are not very long but they are thick and strong and I like to wrap both my arms around one of his when we walk along. It was hard that day though because Robbie was walking faster than normal, and he was swinging from side to side a lot. We went round the back of the flats and straight up to the next floor.

We were at the back of the block. All the flats had their own balcony that side. Robbie was brave. He didn't even think about the danger, he just started climbing along the balconies. From one to the next. I called, "Robbie, wait!" and I followed him. It was scary, really scary, because there was a gap between each balcony, and you could see right down to the ground. Robbie told me to go back but I wouldn't. I was scared back there on my own. I wanted to be with Robbie so I climbed along. I'm not very good at climbing so Robbie helped me, even though he wanted me to go back. He knowed I wouldn't go back though. Every time I climbed over, Robbie had to hold me and pull me by my trousers, and we both fell down. Every time! I giggled, but Robbie didn't. I was scared someone would see us but they didn't. It's funny the things some people keep on their balconies. One of them had two old washing machines and some rusty bikes. One of them had a rabbit hutch full of beer bottles.

When we got to the boy's balcony we could already hear the shouting and the dog barking. There was an ashtray on the balcony and a bowl of water for the dog. Robbie knocked it over when I fell on him. It maked a loud noise. We were scared. We looked in through the window. We could see into their flat through the net curtains. The boy was sitting on the sofa and the lady was shouting at him. We could hear the dog but couldn't see it. The boy had his head down and looked sad. He shouted some things without even looking at her. Then he got up and tried to get past the lady but she wouldn't let him go past. He turned around waving his hands. Then the lady pushed him really hard. He didn't fall over, but she started hitting him. She had gone mad. The boy didn't fight back, he just crouched down and curled up. Then the dog came towards him. It had been behind the sofa. It looked really scared but it was barking at the lady. She screamed at it and it went behind the sofa again, but it didn't stay there. The boy was shouting and trying to get up but the lady kicked him in the face. Then she broke a bowl on his back and he fell to the floor. The dog came out again to help the boy and the lady kicked it. It yowled and barked and she hit it with her hand.

That's when I realised my Robbie was opening the door. He went inside! I saw him in the kitchen, and I watched him going as quickly as he could into the lounge. The lady stopped hitting the boy and looked at my Robbie. Robbie went to help the boy get up. He ignored the lady shouting at him and telling him to get out. The dog came towards him. It was limping. There was lots of noise: shouting and barking, and I was scared and confused.

Then, the woman hit herself in the face. The boy tried to stop her, but she kept doing it. It seemed to go on for ages, the woman hitting herself and the boy and Robbie trying to stop her and the poor dog not knowing what to do. And then the police arrived. One of the neighbours must have called them. They broke the door in! The lady's face was bleeding, and the police grabbed hold of the boy and Robbie. The dog was barking and the woman was shouting, and no-one knowed what was going on. All that time, I was hiding on the balcony. I waited and waited. I was too scared to look. I crouched down and cried.

It was ages and ages before I looked in again. I'd been asleep a bit, and all the shouting had stopped. It was quiet. I didn't know what to do. Robbie had gone. They all had. I was too scared to climb back over the balconies and too scared to go through the house. I just didn't know what to do. And then I remembered I had my phone in my pocket. I rang my mum and she came and got me by going to the flat next door and helping me climb over the balcony.

Mum found out that the police had arrested Robbie. He shouldn't have been in the boy's flat. But the police didn't understand what he was saying to them. So me and Mum went to the police station to explain. I told them about the woman hitting herself and hitting the boy and the dog too. The boy hadn't done anything wrong. Neither had my Robbie. After that, the police let Robbie and the boy go. I was so happy when I saw my Robbie. I don't know where the dog had gone. The boy didn't say anything to us, he just went off in a car with his friends.

I don't think the boy went back to live at his flat after that. The lady did, I saw her. But I didn't see the boy or the dog after that. Not for ages. Not for a really long time. Then one day there was a knock at our door. Robbie opened it. Robbie always answered the door. I was always scared but Robbie wasn't. So Robbie opened the door and I held his arm.

It was the boy. He had his hood up, and he stamped out his cigarette on the pavement. He said, "Alright?" We didn't know what to say. It was embarrassing, a bit. The boy's dog was sitting next to him. The boy said, "I never thanked you. You know, for helping me out." Robbie nodded and looked at the floor. "For helping us both out, me and my dog." I knowed it would be polite to ask the boy in, but I was too shy. I tugged on Robbie's arm and tried to get him to do that but he didn't. "Sorry about my mates, you know, the things they say to you sometimes. I've told them not to anymore. I told them you're alright."

Robbie nodded and I giggled. And I tugged on Robbie's arm and whispered to him to let the boy in. "Anyway, I got you something to say thanks. It's from both of us, me and 'im." The boy pointed at the dog and the dog barked once. Then the boy picked up a box I hadn't noticed. He gived it to Robbie. "It's a puppy. My mate's dog had puppies and I thought you might like one. This dirty old bugger's the father!" His dog barked again. It was like the dog knew what the boy meant. Robbie said, "Thanks," and he gave me the box. I couldn't see because I was crying and I didn't know what to do. I just stood there. "Have a look," said the boy.

Robbie peered into the box. "It's a puppy," he said.

"I know that," said the boy. "D'you wan' 'im? He's for you. A present."

"Yes please," said Robbie. Then the boy came in and helped me put the box on the floor. The puppy was tiny and sleepy.

"I checked with your mum first," the boy said. "She says it's okay, she'll help you look after it."

"And Liz Jones," I said, because Liz Jones would help us too.

The boy gave us two small cans of dog food. "So you don't have to give him Kentucky Fried Chicken," he said, which was funny because that's what we'd told him.

Softly, Gently, Reassuringly

What I can't believe is how long it took me to see it. I have a bit of a knack for seeing things other people can't. And I *am* talking about the supernatural. That's what most people would call it anyway. It just seems really natural to me though. Like the dreams I have when something bad is about to happen. I knew Mum was going to die giving birth to Poppy long before she went into labour, for instance.

"Ruddy milk's sour," Dad said, a disgusted look on his face as he turned to the sink to spit out his Weetabix. "Don't eat it," he snapped at Poppy as she steered an enormous spoonful of Coco Pops into her four-year-old mouth. But she did. Even as Dad took the bowl away from her, she chewed her cereal, milk running down her chin, and said, "It's not sour." Dad inspected her bowl. He sniffed it, then tasted the milk. "Weird," he said. "Yours seems fine. How's yours, Eve?" he asked me. Mine was fine too. So was the milk still in the bottle. But in Dad's bowl, Weetabix lay in milk that had separated into misty, acidic water and cottage cheese.

I should have realised then what was going on.

Later, I watched Poppy playing with her dolls. She had

a teddy which she took everywhere, talking to it in her mumbling, not-yet-fully-formed way, sometimes using real words, sometimes sounding like a Tellytubby. I had my headphones on, and was dozing on the sofa. Justin Timberlake crooned in my head, and I was drowsy with weekend fatigue. I dozed, which was ironic because I had such trouble sleeping at night, but none whatsoever during the day when there was homework and housework to do. And I dreamed that weird dream I'd not had for ages.

A forest, cold, gloomy, with a thick mist which seemed to choke me. I felt a deep, savage fear rising inside me, and I heard my blood thumping through my veins. I knew this place was vile, and hostile, and I knew that there was something for me to see.

A cat with smooth, blonde fur was standing nearby, blinking its big green eyes. We stared at each other, and then, as it always did, it turned away, and I knew I had to follow. Along the path it went, and I struggled to keep up as the overhanging foliage and undergrowth clawed at my clothes and hair. The cat led me deeper and deeper into the darkness of the forest, and my skin crawled with the terror of what might lurk in the heaving shadows and icy hollows so close around me. And then we came upon it, the house in the woods. I knew this house well: it was the image of our own house, the narrow, Victorian terrace, but the rest of the row was not there, and the lone house was derelict. It stank of rotting vegetation and God knows what else. It's windows were dark, the kind of windows you know hold terrifying secrets; the kind you cannot bring yourself to look inside for fear of what you will see; and the icy air drew tight around me, making this feel so real and raw.

I could hear a voice, a man's voice, soft and tender. It was my father's voice. He was telling someone he loved them; he loved them more than he could say. That should have made me feel safe, reassured; I should have been able to run inside the house and find him and embrace him, but I couldn't. It was as if his voice was loaded with a menace which seeped into the air like poison gas, and I was rooted to the spot. The cat approached the house, looking back at me as if beckoning me to follow, but I couldn't. Something terrible was happening in there and I didn't want to see.

And then I was awake, back on the sofa, back in the land of Justin Timberlake and homework, and Poppy playing with her teddy. I pulled my earphones out and let the real world in. How many times had I had that dream? I glanced at Poppy, so innocent, so peaceful in her little world. I listened to her chattering as she fed the teddy invisible cakes, poured invisible tea, read it a meaningless story.

"I love you, Teddy," she said. "I love you more than anything." As she spoke, she fiddled with some stuffing protruding from a hole where Teddy's stitching had come undone. I vowed to sew that up for her. I watched her push the stuffing back in, and then she pushed her fingers right inside. She cupped her hand over Teddy's mouth and said, "Don't tell anyone, Teddy. This can be our secret."

*

How could I have been so slow? How could I not have seen what was right in front of me? It seems so obvious now. But the things going on in our house were things you would never suspect in a million years.

Dad became ill. It seemed that everything he ate was off. I thought at the time it was because his taste buds had gone strange, you know, like when you've got a cold. Dad did have a cold, and he was vomiting a lot too. The doctors could find nothing wrong, and he had good days as well as bad days, but he was starting to look grey around the eyes, and was losing weight. Still they could find nothing. I should have known, but who would ever think of witchcraft?

Poppy barely seemed to notice what was going on. She was unaffected by Dad's illness. She just played with her toys, but I didn't like the way she played. I didn't like the way she whispered things to them, things which sounded so innocent and loving but just felt to me so ... *dangerous*. There was something else going on inside her and I was too afraid to admit I knew what it was. And I didn't want to believe what my father was doing to her. I didn't want to take responsibility for that. The thought of it was too intense and painful for me to comprehend; I couldn't go near it. So, without even realising it, I blocked all of it out.

But Dad got worse. He took days off work, and I nursed him, wishing Mum was here to help. I couldn't bear to see him fade, and worse than that: I couldn't bear the way Poppy looked at him, seeming to understand but not seeming to care. Witchcraft, at her age? It was unthinkable. But, at last, I did begin to think it.

I remember once rocking Poppy in her cradle while she cried. This was a hot summer evening when she was a baby, and there was a fly in the room. It was a big, fat bluebottle, and it kept buzzing my face, irritating the hell out of me. Poppy didn't pay it any attention at all, and she gradually stopped crying and began to doze. But the fly decided it wasn't getting enough attention from me and decided to goad Poppy instead. I tried repeatedly to waft it away from her but it took little notice. And then, suddenly, Poppy's eyes opened, fixed on the fly, and a moment later it dropped out of the air, lifeless.

Later, I found I could do the fly-trick too. It was handy, and scary at the same time. I was older than Poppy, and was wise enough to use it sparingly; I didn't want to hurt flies but sometimes you just need to get rid of them. For years, I'd thought nothing of this. I did realise it wasn't something other kids could do, but it didn't seem to matter that we could; it just meant we never had to put up with flies in our room.

But one day, Dad blustered into the front room, his pyjamas damp with his sweat, and said, "All four apples." Poppy carried on playing, and I asked Dad what he was talking about. I had a sense of dread rising in me, as if I knew what was coming. "Maggots in all of 'em," he said, and showed me the one in his hand. "Everything I touch is rotten or infested with bloody maggots. I feel like I'm cursed."

I looked at Poppy and the room swirled round me in a fug of dismay. My little, tiny sister. Could she really ...? I remembered the dream, the cottage, my father's voice, the menace in it ... I remembered the way Poppy spoke to her toys, the way she acted with them ... I had to face it.

Dad staggered out of the room and into the bathroom. I heard him vomiting. I looked at Poppy. She was looking toward the bathroom in the same intense way she had looked at the fly.

"Stop it," I said to her, feebly. "Poppy, you have to stop this."

"Stop what?" she said, disarming me with an innocent look from those wide, brown eyes.

"Stop what you're doing to Dad," I said, sliding off the sofa and kneeling beside her. She was only four after all, I couldn't be cross with her. Did she even know what she was doing? She needed to be stopped, yes, but she needed to be helped too; she needed to be trained how to control and contain her powers.

"It's not me," she said, gazing up at me now. "It's you."

And the room went icy cold. Poppy was playing again as if nothing had happened, but nothing felt real. My ears were full of an impossible silence. I tried to say something to Poppy but she didn't seem to hear me. She didn't seem to know I was there now, and at the window was that cat, it's bright green eyes imploring me to follow. I knew I had no choice. I opened the front door and, where there should have been garden and road and houses I saw the forest. The cat headed into the mist, and I forced myself to follow. I was dragging myself through muddy air which resisted my every effort, and the trees and briars battled against my progress. I felt I was going to be sick, or cry, or just collapse, but I knew I had to follow the cat to the house in the woods, and somehow, I kept going.

At last the house appeared there in the sticky fog, growing clearer as I approached. My father's voice emanated from a window. The cat, as always, approached the house, imploring me to do the same. This time, I knew I had no choice. The cat leapt up onto the sill of a glassless window, and I knew I had to look inside. My dad was speaking softly, gently, reassuringly, in tones which

149

sent splinters of dread into my throat. I forced myself to look. He was standing over a sleeping figure, leaning over the bed, whispering, pulling back the covers. The figure was too big to be Poppy. It was me, curled up, asleep, under the spell of the sleeping tablets my dad had got me. My father's hand slid over my mouth and he lowered himself onto the bed. Only then did I see Poppy, Teddy in hand, watching from the doorway, unnoticed.

The house, the forest, the dread, vanished. I was in the front room again, and there was Poppy, playing obliviously.

Dad came staggering from the bathroom, hair wild and face wet. He looked at me with an expression of desperation. He leaned against the door jamb, struggling for breath. "What's happening to me?" he said. "Am I dying? Eve, I think I might be dying!"

I could feel Poppy looking up at me. I knew it was me, not her, who was out of control, who had been causing this all along without even knowing it, or knowing why. And I knew I couldn't stop myself.

"Go to bed, Dad," I said, softly, gently, reassuringly. "I'll be up in a minute."

*

After the funeral, we moved in with Auntie Sandra, Mum's sister. I didn't tell anyone what Dad had been doing. I'd not been able to admit it to myself when he was alive, let alone admitting it to other people, even now he was dead. I didn't know how much Poppy remembered, or whether it had affected her in any lasting way. I knew that one day I'd have to talk to her about it, but I wasn't ready yet, and she seemed to be okay. Oddly enough, she never mentioned Dad either.

Somehow, Auntie Sandra seemed to know we didn't want to be reminded of our dad, even though neither of us had said that. So, the photo she hung on the wall in our new bedroom was just of our mum, with her smooth, blonde hair, and green, catlike eyes.

About the Author

David Hall is a pen-name for Antony Wootten. Antony is best known as a children's author and has published several children's books under that name. When writing for adults, he writes under the name David Hall.

If you enjoyed this book, and would be kind enough to recommend it to others, either by telling them about it or by writing a review online somewhere, Antony would be extremely grateful. So would I.

Thank you.
David Hall.

Also by David Hall:

Gordon Medley's Final Frontier
England, 1989. Star Trek fan Gordon Medley accidentally becomes embroiled in an epic tale of planetary destruction, out-of-control super-computers, and time-travel. And throughout his voyage of self-discovery, he is faced with a question which he cannot begin to answer: why are all the people he meets so similar to the characters in Star Trek?

www.antonywootten.co.uk/davidhall.html

Children's books by Antony Wootten:

A Tiger Too Many

Jill is deeply fond of an elderly tiger in London Zoo. But when war breaks out, she makes a shocking discovery. For reasons she can barely begin to understand, the tiger, along with many other animals in the zoo, is about to be killed. She vows to prevent that from happening, but finds herself virtually powerless in an adults' world. That day, she begins a war of her own, a war to save a tiger.

Grown-ups Can't Be Friends With Dragons

Brian is always in trouble at school, and his home life is far from peaceful. So he often runs away to the cave by the sea where he has happy memories. But there is something else in the cave: a creature, lonely and confused. Together they visit another world where they find wonderful friends, but also deadly enemies. Brian's life is torn between the two worlds, and he begins to believe that, in his own world at least, grown-ups can't be friends with dragons.

There Was An Old Fellow From Skye

A collection of Antony's hilarious limericks for all the family to enjoy. Featuring everything from King Arthur and his knights to inter-stellar space-travel, There Was An Old Fellow From Skye is packed with tiny tales which will tickle the ribs of children and adults alike.

www.antonywootten.co.uk